"As the challenged, it is my privilege to dictate the form and nature of the duel," Kamchan announced. And then he let fall the
first thunderbolt he had been saving. *"It shall
be in the form of a game of Darza, fought between Koja of the Kandars and myself, the
Darza pieces to be represented by living men
and women, of my selection."*

A murmur of consternation and surprise ran
over the room.

Then Kamchan let fall a second thunderbolt.

"The captives, together with the outlaw
Borak, shall serve, O Koja, as your living
Darza pieces," he said gloatingly.

Koja said nothing.

The captives who would fight in this game of
living Callistan chess were none other than
Prince Valkar, Princess Xara, Kadar of Shondakor, and little Taran.

And the game would be—*to the death.*

RENEGADE
OF CALLISTO

LIN CARTER

A DELL BOOK

Published by
Dell Publishing Co., Inc.
1 Dag Hammarskjold Plaza
New York, New York 10017

Dell ® TM 681510, Dell Publishing Co., Inc.

ISBN: 0-440-14377-2

Printed in the United States of America
First printing—August 1978

RENEGADE OF CALLISTO
is dedicated to OTIS ADELBERT KLINE,
ROY ROCKWOOD, and WILLIAM L. CHESTER,
the best of the earlier writers who contributed
so much to "The Burroughs Tradition."

Contents

RENEGADE
OF CALLISTO

THANATOR
THE JUNGLE MOON

NOR[T]

The FROZE[N]

Zanadar

THE WHITE MOUNTAI[NS]

The GRAND KUM[A]

THE GATE

SANMUR LAJ, the Lesser Sea

The PLAIN[S]

SOU[TH]

Lin Carter

Introduction

A Message from Another World

It had been about a year and a half since my wife and I had returned from our visit to Cambodia, when the mailman delivered the manuscript which I have edited into the book you are now holding in your hands.

Our brief visit to Sir Malcolm Jerrolds's dig at the site of the Arangkôr excavations I have elsewhere described. But since our return home we had unfortunately lost touch with the peppery and persistent British archaeologist. Nothing came our way but brief, maddeningly fragmentary scraps of news. The collapse of the shaky Lon Nol regime and the subsequent takeover of the Cambodian government by the insurgent forces was adequately described in the news media, of course; but the fate of our friend we were forced to piece together from snippets of rumor and hearsay.

Along with all other British, American, and French nationals then resident in that war-torn little corner of Southeast Asia, he had been evacuated to safety by two American destroyers. Most embassy personnel had been flown out of the country about the same time, when the Communist takeover seemed imminent, so there was no one we could contact there who would tell us anything about what had become of him.

For these reasons, then, it was with enormous relief that I weighed the bulky package in my hands, recognizing by his ungainly scribble the sender of the package. Within, I found a scrawled note in his hand which at once answered many questions that had long plagued me. Sir Malcolm had been flown by helicopter, together with other foreign nationals, to the destroyers waiting at the mouth of the Mekong Delta. From there he had been taken by ship to a friendly port and was put up for a time in the British embassy. Eventually, he flew to London, squabbling with Foreign Office officials from whom he demanded a renewal of his visa and approval from the new government of Cambodia so that he could return to the site of the Arangkôr dig to resume his work.

Apparently, however, the new government was reluctant to admit foreign visitors until (I suppose) they completed the process of cementing the transfer of power—which is to say, the swift trial and elimination of as many fugitive members of the former government as they could get their hands on. Jerrolds then went home to Edinburgh to sulk and fume until these matters were concluded and no cause remained for the new regime to refuse admittance to foreigners.

He got back to Arangkôr, of course, in the end. It would take more than a few hostile armies or suspicious and xenophobic governments to keep such as Sir Malcolm away from his work for very long. And, once back at the Lost City in the Cambodian jungles, he found another manuscript awaiting him at the bottom of that mysterious jade-lined well that forms the link between our own Earth and the distant world of Thanator, or Callisto, fifth moon of far-off Jupiter.

As has been the case with six previous books in this series, I have confined myself to making merely editorial revisions in the manuscripts thus received from the lone American soldier-of-fortune whom Destiny or Chance has transported to that far planet. That is, I have corrected errors in grammar or spelling or punctuation wherever I have noticed them, christened the book with a title of my own devising, and titled each chapter.

Six books, I say, have I transcribed, before I began work on this one. The seventh, of course, is entirely of my own authoring—*Lankar of Callisto*. I weary of repeating, in such introductions as this, the plain and simple fact that, with the sole exception of *Lankar*, I am but the editor, not the author, of these volumes.

—LIN CARTER
Hollis, Long Island, New York

BOOK ONE

TARAN,
SKY CADET

Masters of the Upper Air

Human ingenuity is the crowning marvel of all Creation.

And, of all the works of man's invention, I regard the unique and unparalleled ornithopters of Thanator as among the more ingenious and remarkable.

To conceive of the very notion of a flying machine in a society whose science has yet to progress beyond something resembling the High Renaissance is in itself remarkable. And it would have seemed even more remarkable to me had not the mighty brain of Leonardo—that titan intellect of the Renaissance—duplicated the feat of the unsung and nameless Callistan engineer who first conceived of the ornithopter. For the Florentine superman himself dreamed of a flying machine that flew as a bird flies—by flapping its wings. But some Callistan genius actually perfected the concept, from its initial visualization to the physical reality.

It was lifting gas, found only in the White Mountains, that made the dream of weightless flight come true. Sometimes I wonder whether, had hydrogen or helium been known in the Florence of Leonardo da

Vinci, the age of flight might not have begun centuries before the Wright brothers.

When my friends and I succeeded in destroying for all time the power of the cruel and rapacious Sky Pirates of Zanadar, we wrote finis to their unchecked reign as masters of the upper air. And from the ruination of their buccaneering kingdom we carried off the secrets of constructing the sky-ships. Thought and experiment and a certain amount of luck had enabled my people of Shondakor to construct a Sky Navy: now we were the masters of the upper sky, Lords of the Air.

The Golden City of Shondakor enjoys a kindly and beneficent reign over the kingdoms of Thanator. Its rulers are not likely to employ their new airfleet to conquer or subject neighboring realms. I can say this with utter certitude, and a degree of pride as well, for I and my beloved Princess, Darloona, are the rulers of Shondakor.

The sky-ships are immense and ungainly, albeit weightless, and require the strength of human muscles, or the lucky direction of the winds, to give them motive power. Even the little four-man gigs must be pedaled—for all the world like airborne bicycles!—in order to fly. And this has long bothered me: this discrepancy between the technological marvel of the huge flying ships themselves and the primitive muscle power required to move them about the sky.

I could see no reason why some form of lightweight engine could not be added to their structure to drive the jointed and mobile vans. And I had long intended to seek sufficient leisure in which to tinker up such a device, as yet unconceived even by the most advanced Callistan genius.

But, alas, the rulers of cities oft have many weighty burdens to occupy their time, and leisure is a rare commodity for kings. Making just and needed laws, enforcing them with alacrity and even-handedness, establishing tax rates (and collecting them), dispensing justice, hearing the argument of suits, studying petitions, overseeing the various governmental offices, officiating at ceremonial functions, laying cornerstones, rewarding loyal service and punishing the venal—these and a thousand other bothersome duties add weight to the burden of a crown, and a ruler dares to delegate his authority only so much and no more.

But once the power of the insidious Mind Wizards had been crushed, and we had returned from our long wars on the Far Side of Thanator, my kingdom entered upon one of those golden times kings dream of. Peace reigned, and Shondakor was at enmity with no other nation or people. Trade flourished, since we had newly entered into close and cooperative alliance with our neighboring cities, Soraba and Tharkol, and an abundance of wealth and prosperity flowed through our gates.

Thus it was that I seized the advantage offered by this brief, prosperous, peaceful period in Shondakor's history and turned my attention to the reinvention of the airplane engine. Since I had long been an aviator on my native world, I didn't think that the project could be other than simple and easy.

Well, it proved a lot more difficult than I had imagined. It is one thing to be able to order pistons and fuel tanks, propeller blades and spark plugs from the nearest supply house, and quite another to try to describe them to a bunch of bewildered Renaissance craftsmen and artisans!

Take, for example, that plain and lowly device, the simple spark plug. What, exactly, goes inside the damned thing? What is it *made* of?—how much goes in?—how is it processed?—what are the sizes and weights and proportions of each component?—and the *precise* sizes, weights, and proportions, if you please!

Reinventing the airplane engine meant I had to reinvent a hundred other gadgets first, and the tools to make them, too. For many months I kept the craftsmen, artisans, and ironsmiths of Shondakor, Tharkol, and Soraba busy, busy, busy, putting together engines that blew up, caught fire, or did nothing but sit there like mere dead lumps of metal.

A thousand times I would readily have given it all up for just one of the primitive little gas-gulpers that drove the Wright brothers' box kite at Kitty Hawk. But, constantly redesigning for something lighter in weight and less complex, I persevered. And, eventually, success was mine.

The problem went beyond merely building the tools and the parts; the trouble lay in the fact that the lifting gas contained in the double hull was ferociously explosive and flammable, and the hull itself was only heavy paper laminated with coat after coat of baked-on glue. One spark from the engine and we would have a flying torch! I had to devise a way of keeping the engine out of contact with the hull of the craft, and eventually I came up with the notion of hanging it on the tail, mounted by means of a metal bracket. This way, any sparks that went flying out in the black smoke would be whipped away by the slipstream behind the sky-ship.

It was crude—and it was complicated—but it worked!

The Sky Navy of the Three Cities by this period consisted of some eight of these flying ships. Among these were the *Xaxar* and the *Jalathadar*, which had been salvaged from the destruction of Zanadar, and the *Zarkoon*, the *Avenger*, the *Arkonna*, and the *Conqueress*, which had been constructed in the shipyards of Tharkol. My country had its own shipyards by this time, and our two new vessels, the *Shondakor* and the *Darloona*, completed the fleet.

Still more vessels were under construction at Tharkol and in Shondakor, in a variety of new designs. Among these were some purely mercantile transport ships financed by the merchants of Soraba, and a squadron of small, speedy scout-vessels which would be employed to patrol our mutual borders.

Naturally, once my engine was perfected, the older ships were outfitted with the new invention and their old, cumbersome apparatus of hand-turned wheel systems was removed from the mid-deck hold. And all of the ships newly built or currently under construction would automatically be fitted with the "Jandar engine," as it had been named.

Until a new modern squadron of scouts was ready to be launched, we employed the old four-man gigs for that purpose. These curious vessels resembled outrigger canoes with rigid wings: they were small, light, speedy, and maneuverable. Their supplies of lifting gas were strictly limited, because scouts could carry only a light cargo. Young, relatively lightweight Shondakorian cadets were therefore trained to fly them, usually boys in their teens.

One of the cadets was Taran, the little jungle boy Prince Lankar had rescued from the web of the giant spider in the Grand Kumala, and whom he had brought along with him to Shondakor. The bright, good-natured, likable lad soon made many good friends, and after Prince Lankar returned home to his—and my—native planet, Earth, little Taran stayed in Shondakor and was enlisted as a cadet in the legions of the Golden City. When we began to train a cadre of young officers for the Sky Navy, the lad begged to join their ranks, and thus Taran of the Ku Thad became a sky cadet.

When Prince Lankar first encountered Taran in the jungle country, the child was about twelve—slender of build, with coltish legs and a sturdy chest and shoulders, emerald eyes twinkling mischievously under an unruly mop of red-gold curls, with a full-lipped, childish mouth whose softness was belied by the resolute and manly set of his jaw. But by the period of which I write he was nearly fourteen, a tall, long-legged youth who had not lost his boyish sense of pranksome fun, but had added to it a more serious sense of responsibility.

We had all grown immensely fond of Taran. In-deed, it was not possible to resist for very long his good humor and playfulness, and the very genuine earnestness with which he tackled every task that came before him. Since he was an orphan, and there-fore a Ward of the Throne, all of us at court more or less adopted him and vied with each other for the pleasure of his company. Sir Tomar, who was not all that much older than he, had been as a brother to the boy; but now that Tomar and Ylana of the Jungle Country were wed and had become the parents of twins, it was Koja and Ergon and Lukor and I who served *in loco parentis;* too much older to be like brothers, I fear, we were regarded by him as affec-tionate and indulgent uncles, nothing more. His heart he had given only to Prince Lankar the Earthling, who had rescued him from the *ximchak*'s web. But of us all I believe young Taran loved Koja the best.

On the surface of it, there was absolutely nothing about either of the two to draw them together. Koja, of course, being a Yathoon Hordesman, was not even human: the people of the Hordes are true arthropods, insect-men, tall, gaunt, ungainly, their stalking limbs clad in horny gray chitin, their heads expressionless masks of horn with knobbed antennae and great compound eyes like clusters of black jewels. Cold, emotionless, devoid of sentiment, they are ferocious warriors, implacable foes, enemies of all men.

It is a matter of particular pride to me that, of all the men and women who have ever walked the surface of Thanator the Jungle Moon, I was the first to make friends with a warrior of the Yathoon Horde. Of this rare accomplishment I have written at length in another portion of these journals,* so I shall not describe here the combination of patience, cultivation, luck, and sheer accident by which the miracle was accomplished. Suffice it to say that, once I had shared with Koja the true meaning of friendship, he discovered for himself the meaning of love. And, of all the hundreds of comrades and friends I have made during the years of my sojourn upon this fifth moon of Jupiter, none, with the royal exception of my beloved Princess, lies closer to my heart than the solemn arthropod whose slave and possession I once was.

Of all that brave and stalwart company, no more true and loyal friend have I than Koja, whose selfless dedication and love for me I am proud and privileged to return.

On the surface of things, it seemed highly unlikely that Koja and Taran, being worlds apart, would become the closest of friends. But friends they did indeed become, despite the gulf that yawned between them, the differences of age, race, and personality. The reason for their closeness may have sprung, in fact, from these very differences—for neither Taran nor Koja had been reared here in Shondakor, and were thus strangers from distant lands; in addition, both were unique—Koja, being the only Yathoon in captivity, so to speak, and Taran, much younger than any of the others at court. Perhaps their aloneness drew them together.

In the eyes of young Taran—still the eyes of a boy—the gaunt, solemn, humorless Yathoon was the most fascinating of playmates—it was as if a child of my race could have for a friend Winnie the Pooh or Reepicheep or the Tin Woodsman of Oz. And Koja,

* Here Jon Dark obviously refers to the first volume of his memoirs, which I edited for publication under the title of *Jandar of Callisto*.

I knew, had developed a warmly protective feeling for the children of our race. His own kind mate but never marry, and do not rear their young personally, but in a far and secret place near the South Pole of the planet, a realm they regard with superstitious veneration as holy for some reason I have never known. Our custom of raising our children in family groups seems strange to such as Koja; having observed the love and affection we humans share between child and parent, I believe he envies us and yearns, in the depths of his unknowable heart, to share in that closest of all bonds.

I know that my own little son, Prince Kaldar, now a chubby and tireless little rascal of two and a half, crows with delight whenever Koja is near, laughs delightedly at his solemn voice and expressionless face, loves to be bounced on his gaunt and bony lap, and breathlessly confides his every childish escapade or mishap to his "Uncle Koja." So the fondness which grew between Koja and Taran came as no particular surprise to me.

You never saw anything as amusing, or as touching, as the two of them together. Tall and long-legged as Taran is, the gigantic insectoid towers to twice his height; and when Koja exercises the boy in the art of the blade, two more unequal adversaries could not be imagined. Koja's sword, a true Yathoon whip-sword, is longer than Taran is tall!

I have smiled at the sight of them strolling on the esplanade or in the palace gardens or on the terraces, talking together confidentially in low tones, the towering stilt-legged Yathoon gently holding the trusting boy's hand in his powerful armored grasp, his expressionless head bent to observe the lad's excited, mobile face and sparkling eyes, carefully replying to the boy's torrent of eager questions or complaints in cold, toneless, and metallic monosyllables.

How wonderful a miracle is love! For it can bring

together the most different of creatures, though they truly be worlds apart.

Most recently, a third partner has entered into the close friendship that exists between Koja and Taran. I refer to that waddling and bowlegged purple-furred monstrosity with a huge and faithful heart of purest gold, Bozo the *othode*.

Again, as was the case with Taran himself, it was Prince Lankar who befriended the burly-chested beast in the Grand Kumala. On his home world and in his private life, my Earthling friend has a fondness for dogs. And when he was here among us on Callisto, however briefly, Lankar would not have been Lankar had he not made friends with the mighty *othode*— Thanator's closest equivalent to something resembling a bull mastiff grown larger than a Great Dane, fitted out with a few extra legs, a grinning, froglike mouth that gawps from ear to ear, and goggling eyes like a gigantic Peke.

I suspect that, of all the friends he made here on Callisto, the one he most hated to part from was Bozo.* While we were escorting Prince Lankar to the Callistan terminus of the Gateway Between Two Worlds, and while the Prince was fretting over how to say good-bye to his immense friend, Bozo—or was it Nature?—solved the problem for him. For it would seem the mating season for *othodes* had come, and the huge beast responded with as much alacrity to the Call of the Wild as ever did Buck the wolf-dog in the pages of Jack London's excellent novel.

I later sent a message to my friend back on Earth, informing him that we had seen Bozo and his mate, together with a litter of eight of the fattest, most adorable *othode* pups imaginable. Well, it would seem

* My acquaintance with Bozo the *othode* I have described in *Lankar of Callisto*, the sixth book in this series.

that *othodes* do not mate for life, because in the interim Mrs. Bozo has gone back to the wild, with most of her litter, and Bozo, together with one of his male pups, feeling the need for human companionship again, now that the urge for domesticity had waned, took to haunting the gates of Shondakor, and finally deigned to join us in the palace as a pet of the entire court.

On the whole, the Ku Thad generally do not adopt pets. *Othodes,* however, long ago formed a sort of truce with the Golden People which is similar to that which was long ago arranged back on Earth during the early Ice Age, when the first man made friends with the first dog. That is to say, my people train *othodes* for hunting. Generally, the beasts are used in hunting packs, but it is not entirely unknown for a single human hunter to work game in comradeship with a lone *othode.* At any rate, my courtiers were already fond of Bozo—for it was none other than the faithful Bozo who had found the hidden door to Kúur, and because of his keen nose and hunting instinct, we found and crushed the dread and dangerous Mind Wizards. Hence Bozo was more than tolerated. Indeed, he was loved. And so was his son, an awkward and ungainly half-grown pup I had christened Fido, because "Fido, son of Bozo" has a nice ring to it.

Bozo likes me very much—but he *loves* Taran, since the boy had been with Lankar almost from the very first. While in the palace, Bozo sleeps wherever he likes, sometimes in the suite I share with my beloved Darloona, sometimes on hot nights in the cool gardens—but, more often than not, he chooses to share the little bed on which Taran sleeps when he is not on duty in the cadet barracks.

The boy and the waddling pair of *othodes* remained close friends even after Taran left the legion to serve with the sky cadets.

And it is entirely because of this simple fact that the most surprising adventure occurred, whereby the fate of many thousands was changed, and the destinies of nations were forever altered. . . .

2

The Runaways

On a lazy afternoon, following flight practice, Taran brought his little gig down to one of the rooftop mooring masts and expertly anchored the craft into position with a deft twist of the mooring cable. The cable was a light but strong length of line with a small, collapsible grappling hook attached to it—rather like a miniature anchor for this little ship of the skies.

The mooring mast itself was one of the several that thrust skyward from one of the middle tiers of the royal palace. Here were anchored the skycraft of various officers and courtiers, messengers with important dispatches, and similar functionaries. The young sky cadet was actually supposed to return his craft to its berth at the huge skydrome on the other side of Shondakor, near the shipyards. But the boy wished to demonstrate his new facility to his friend Koja, whose suite of apartments was situated in this part of the palace.

Taran found Koja with Bozo and Fido, returning from a spell of exercise in the palace gardens. *Othodes* had first been domesticated by the Yathoon warriors, who used them for hunting and tracking, and Koja

had taken unto himself the enjoyable task of training
the two waddling brutes to come at command and to
obey simple orders.

Actually, it wasn't Taran who found Bozo and
Fido, it was really Bozo and Fido who found Taran.
The beasts had an extraordinary sense of smell and
detected the approach of their little friend and play-
mate long before he knew they were about. Whuffing
and snorting vigorously, the two *othodes* came bounding up to the lad and cavorted happily about him,
leaping up to lick his face. Fido, like the overgrown
puppy he was, kept trying to snatch a mouthful of
the short, hip-length cloak the boy wore, in order to
play a rather one-sided game of tug-of-war.

Koja followed the two Callistan hounds as they
went bounding off toward the terrace, and came up
to them to find the boy hugging and petting the two
brutes, who stared up into his face with love in their
eyes, showing grins that stretched from ear to ear, and
striving desperately to wag their tails as dogs would.
Nature failed to equip *othodes* with tails, and their
efforts were not only futile but also exceedingly com-
ical to watch. You really have to see for yourself an
othode trying to wag a tail that isn't there.

His features an impassive mask as always, Koja
surveyed the healthy, long-legged boy from head to
foot, approving of what he saw. In fact, the stalk-
legged arthropod was beaming fondly upon the boy,
although you would never have guessed this from the
cold glitter of his enormous eyes or the rigor of his
expression.

"You look like a real sky cadet today, little Taran,"
remarked the insect-man in his grating, metallic tones.
He had not before seen the boy in full-dress uniform,
winged silver helm, short cloak of sparkling silvery
fabric, close-fitting sky-blue trousers tucked into calf-
high silvered-leather boots, and deep blue tunic em-
blazoned over the heart with the Shondakorian

emblem. The boy grinned back at the arthropod, flushed and happy.

"Do I *really* look good, Koja-*chan*?" he asked, spreading his cloak with both hands and gazing down to admire himself in all his resplendance. Words tumbling all over themselves, Taran told his solemn friend that he had just come from a special display of practice put on for Kaamurath of Soraba, then visiting Jandar and Darloona on a tour of state. The friendly Seraan of neighboring Soraba was here to purchase some scoutcraft of his own.

". . . an' Glypto was there, too!" the lad finished breathlessly. Koja nodded jerkily; he had known of the state visit of the Soraban monarch, but had avoided attending the festivities as such occasions he found a dreary bore. Indeed, they usually are—but little boys find little in life that bores them aside from lessons.

He turned from his contemplation of Taran's military finery to admire the little gig as it wobbled and bobbled at the end of its mooring cable. Sleek and trim it was, a slender, tapering projectile with open cabin and four bucket-seats, like a canoe, riding the breeze on its airtight pontoons. It was in these twin cylinders that the levitating gas was pent. From wingtip to rudder, the sleek little aircraft had been painted in blue and silver, with the blazon of Shondakor on the left side on its prow. Just above the insignia, a neat row of scarlet characters had been inscribed.

Koja did not know that Taran had been privileged to name his own gig—an honor reserved for the upper percentile of cadets—and leaned forward to read the lettering.

"I call it after Lankar-*jan*," sighed the boy, a momentary expression of wistfulness dimming his ardor. "I do miss him so, Koja."

"I know," observed the Yathoon. "So does Bozo— look at him."

Taran giggled. The burly *othode* had leaped up on the top of the parapet and now stood with his hind legs on the wall and his front paws hooked over the lip of the cockpit, sniffing the seat eagerly. Fido scrambled and cavorted about in an agony of frustrated curiosity beneath.

"Yes—I forgot!—I brought them a snack from the welcoming feast—"

Bozo found the haunch of meat hidden beneath the pilot's seat, however, all by himself, and hopped clumsily down to waddle away with his treat, growling at his son in such a manner as to suggest "This is my snack—go find your own!", which was greedy of him, but not at all unothodelike.

Taran ran after the older *othode*, scolding him and trying to take away the meat so as to make him share it with Fido. Koja stood watching, his back turned to the skycraft, and he would have chuckled tolerantly, had nature designed him for chuckling, which it hadn't.

While neither of them was looking, Fido decided to investigate the pilot's seat on his own. Disappointed in not being allowed to share in the treat, the ungainly pup obviously wished to determine if any further goodies reposed in the craft.

The pup had watched how his father had jumped up on the parapet and then stood on his hind legs while holding onto the edge of the cockpit with his forepaws. Now the pup repeated this sequence of actions, somewhat more clumsily and more gracelessly than had Bozo, but without accident. However, there was the matter of that *middle* set of legs! Fido could not quite remember how his father had disposed of them, so he hooked them into the cockpit, too.

With the natural result that, when the first gust of wind came to make the *Lankar-jan* wobble from side to side, Fido found his hind legs losing contact with the parapet, and in the next moment the *othode*

discovered himself hanging onto the edge of the cockpit, with the rest of him dangling in thin air.

On occasions such as this, when his inquisitive or
mischievous ways had gotten him into trouble, the
pup had learned to call for assistance. So Fido raised
his voice in a mournful howl, while clinging to the
cockpit for dear life, kicking and scrabbling with his
hind legs for something to stand on.

Eventually, he found the pontoon. Standing on it,
however, made the craft veer half over in a sickening
way. So the pup did the only sensible thing under the
circumstances, and half-clambered, half-fell into the
cockpit.

At the first unhappy yowl, Bozo pricked up his ears
and saw the trouble his bothersome pup had gotten
into. He promptly dropped the bone and went racing
to where the unhappy Fido sat in the pilot's seat. With
a gasp of horror, Taran saw the pup's danger—and
also the horrible chance that the terrified *othode*
might damage the skycraft entrusted to his care—and
sprinted to help Fido out of his predicament. Koja
was at his heels, but Taran reached the craft first.

Jumping up, the boy caught the mooring line and,
clambering along it as agile as any monkey, climbed
into the *Lankar-jan* from the rear. And just then the
Unpredictable happened—

If it hadn't, of course, the events described in this
book might never have occurred, and this book would
never have been written.

But it did, and it was. And thereby hangs a tale . . .

Two things followed, both almost at the same time.

In the first place, Taran had apparently not been
quite as deft as he had thought when he snagged the
mooring mast with the grappling hook. There is an art
to mooring a gig—a clever twist of the wrist when you
toss out the mooring cable—and it is not unlike the

deft twist you must give in throwing out a lasso. An expert lasso-tosser is adept at doing this properly.

Taran now proved, if not actually careless, at least somewhat less than adept. For when he clambered into the rear of the *Lankar-jan,* he joggled the craft rudely.

And the anchor came undone.

Before Taran or Koja or even Fido knew what had happened, the little skycraft went floating off away from the tier until it was drifting out over the streets of the city.

And the only one in the pilot's seat was Fido. At any moment, the frantically wriggling *othode* might touch a lever or push a pedal and start the engine. If this happened, the little craft would fly off under power with no one at the controls—perhaps to hurtle into the side of a building, or to turn upside down and pitch its two young occupants to their death.

What Koja did then he did too swiftly to have considered the potential consequences of his action. It must have been sheer instinct—the innate urge of the mature to protect their young.

Springing to the edge of the tier, he threw himself into space!

His arms were longer than those of a human being, his body much lighter, and his double-jointed rear limbs packed more than human strength and were capable of fantastic leaps.

For these reasons, then, I suppose, instead of falling to his death on the stone pavement far below, he actually managed to catch hold of the rear strut of the left pontoon.

Dangling by his claw-tips, with the rest of his body dangling above the rooftops, Koja let the drifting craft carry him where it would.

Fido raised an unhappy yowl as this additional weight made the rear of the skycraft sag alarmingly, while the nose lifted steeply heavenward. And in his panic, the pup stepped on that pedal after all.

The engine coughed once, then roared into life.

And the *Lankar-jan*, pointed giddily skyward, soared into the zenith without a human hand at the controls!

The wind tugged at his cloak and whipped his face with an invisible lash that made his cheeks sting and his eyes tear. Taran was dreadfully frightened, but there was no time for such feelings now. So the brave boy forgot all about his fears and climbed over into the front seat and proceeded to attempt to pry the panicky pup from the controls.

Perhaps this sounds easy, but the doing of it proved difficult. Poor Fido was nearly scared out of his wits (such as they were!), and he clung desperately to Taran with all six legs. For another thing, even though he was only half-grown, a half-grown *othode* is still a lot of beast.

It took a bit of doing, but Taran eventually managed to lift Fido out of the pilot's seat and drag him into the rear seats where, presumably, the panicky pup could do no harm.

By this time Koja had caught hold of the edge of the cockpit. He hauled himself into the craft and helped the boy to immobilize the *othode*. All four seats had been fitted out with safety belts—such small, light craft can easily be capsized by a sudden gust of air, being virtually weightless—and it was not long before the two succeeded in fastening one of the rear safety belts to the collar Fido wore, using the belt as a makeshift leash.

Once this was accomplished, Taran climbed into the pilot's seat and began to examine the controls. The craft was still climbing into the sky at a steep angle, but the young cadet managed to work the ailerons and tailfin rudder in such a way as to bring the *Lankar-jan*'s nose down and elevate the tail until the craft was flying on an even keel again.

It had, however, ascended to a considerable altitude

by that point and the air was bitterly cold. Worse than that was the fact that Shondakor no longer lay beneath them. The Golden City of the Ku Thad was, in fact, no longer visible below.

Taran stared around him, searching the horizon with eyes tightly narrowed so they would not water in the wind. Afternoon had become darkness quite suddenly, as was the way of things on Callisto where "daylight" does not depend on radiation from the sun, and such phenomena as sunset and twilight are, therefore, unknown. It was pitch-dark below them and even Taran's sharp young eyes could discern no particular feature of the night-shrouded landscape as it rushed past beneath them.

"Is everything all right with the machine?" inquired Koja quietly. The young sky cadet shook his head wordlessly, trying to think.

Their predicament was a peculiar one. Taran knew they could not possibly be more than just a few minutes' flying time from the city of the Ku Thad, but he had absolutely no idea in which direction the city might lie. The trouble was that, during those first few crucial moments when the aircraft had been soaring into the heavens above Shondakor, they had both been too busy trying to get Fido tied down to notice in which direction the runaway ornithopter was heading.

The craft bore nothing on its instrument panel to serve in lieu of a compass, and, as the Thanatorians have never learned to ascertain direction from the stars, Taran was helpless to know which way to turn. At this very moment, they might indeed be flying back to Shondakor; on the other hand, it was equally possible that every consecutive instant of flying time could be carrying them farther and farther from the city. What was he to do?

Incidentally, the reason why the races native to Thanator do not possess much knowledge of the skies is due, quite simply, to the fact that their world is part of the Jovian moon-system. When you share the heavens with a dozen or so major luminaries, stars and constellations are not all that easily visible. And the orbits of the moons of Jupiter are excessively complicated—and the situation is further complicated by the fact that the Thanatorian races live on the surface of one of those moons, in the very midst of the system.

Trying to think of something to do, Taran took the controls tentatively. And the *Lankar-jan* hurtled on, careening blindly through the impenetrable darkness.

Behind, on the parapet of the palace, Bozo stared after the hurtling craft. The mighty *othode* knew in the depths of his faithful and loyal heart that something was very wrong, but he did not know precisely what. He knew, however, that Taran and Koja and Fido were somehow in trouble, in danger, and the great beast threw back his head and lifted his voice in a hoarse, despairing howl.

Then he turned, left the tier, and went waddling down the inner stairs of the palace as fast as his six bowlegs could move—which was quite fast.

The courtiers and guards were accustomed to seeing the burly *othode* trotting here and there by now and paid him no particular attention. Nor did Bozo chance to encounter one of his particular human friends, such as Lukor or myself. Hence he did not attempt to convey what had chanced to occur, but, ignoring the humans he encountered on his way through the palace, Bozo left the immense edifice by the nearest exit and galloped through the parks and gardens, soon gaining the streets of the city beyond.

The worried beast had noted the direction in which the ornithopter had been flying when it had receded into the distant sky, dwindling from his view. Now every instinct of his brave and loyal heart urged him to follow the craft in which his friends and his son were being carried off.

Within a few minutes Bozo was out of the city entirely.

He paused on the outskirts, then waddled through the nearest gate, peered long and earnestly into the darkness that by now had mantled the broad and level Plains of Haratha, and then, stretching his six powerful legs into an easy and tireless lope, the *othode* began to chase the flying craft on foot.

There was nothing else for Bozo to do. And he knew with his every instinct that he must do something.

The sentinels at that gate saw and recognized Bozo as a palace pet; they saw him go loping off into the night but thought nothing of it.

Later—much later—they had reason to regret their inattention.

3

Lost in the Sky

Taran was frightened. The boy had not been this frightened in a long time, not since he and Bozo had taken part in the attack on Kúur, the underground citadel of the Mind Wizards on the Far Side of Callisto. But he tried not to show it.

Fate, it seemed, had played one last trick upon them. It was bad enough to be lost in the skies, without knowing which way to go. What made it so much worse was the fact that they could not control the direction of their flight, even if they *had* known!

For as soon as the sky cadet attempted to work the controls, he discovered that they no longer worked. The control cables had snapped, which meant that he could no longer exert any influence over the direction or altitude of their flight.

Obviously, in his frantic scrambling about, Fido had broken the cables. Nor could they be repaired while they were still aloft, Taran knew. Like all other Shondakorian sky cadets, he had been taught how to make emergency repairs—but these could only be made when the skycraft was at rest.

The reason why this was obligatory was very simple:

you had to climb under the skycraft and rethread or reconnect the cables from beneath.

When he conveyed this dispiriting information to Koja, the solemn Yathoon counseled him not to worry.

"Things are never quite as bad as you at first assume them to be," the arthropod pointed out in his toneless, metallic voice. "We are at present in two different kinds of danger. The first of these is that we have become lost and do not know which is the direction in which we desire to go. This is, however, only a temporary predicament. With daylight we shall be able to ascertain our approximate position on the surface of Thanator from the surface features visible to us."

"I don't see how we can be—"

"I mean that if, by day, we find ourselves flying over jungles, we shall know that we are over the Grand Kumala, and are therefore due west of Shondakor. And, should we find ourselves flying over a vast body of water, we shall thereby know that we have flown due east, and are over the Corund Laj."

"I see what you mean," the boy said seriously. "And if we're over grasslands, it's the Great Plains of Haratha, right?"

"Correct," nodded Koja with a stiff little jerk of his horny head. "Similarly, if we find ourselves in the vicinity of a city, the chances are excellent that we shall be able to recognize it, either from the surroundings or from the city's appearance. And, whether we are over Tharkol or Soraba or Ganatol, or even Narouk or Farz or great Perushtar itself, we shall know exactly where we are in relation to Shondakor the Golden. It is quite impossible for us to become really lost, as long as we keep our wits about us."

The young cadet nodded thoughtfully and began to relax just a bit as his consternation subsided. Koja stole a furtive glance at the boy sideways, but said nothing. Actually, he was nowhere near as certain that they could not become thoroughly lost as his soothing words seemed to suggest. He had been striving to calm the boy's fears so as to spare him needless worry. So he had not exactly been candid with Taran in his estimate of their difficulties.

If, with day, they found themselves over water, for example, it could as easily be the Sanmur Laj as the Corund Laj—and these bodies, the two seas of Callisto, lay at opposite ends of the world.

And should they find themselves flying over the level grasslands, these would indeed be the Great Plains of Haratha: but the Great Plains cover many thousands of square miles—and any one of these square miles looks much like another.

They flew on into the darkness, not speaking.

After a time a fleck of golden flame rose above the horizon. This, they knew, was Juruvad—the "Little Moon"—which we know as Amalthea. And before long a jade luminance painted the dim horizon with pallid emerald fire. This was another of the many moons of mighty Jupiter, and much larger: Orovad, the Callistans call it, but to us it is Io, the second moon.

Within half an hour the dark landscape was illuminated by a much larger spheroid, of frosty azure, which we call Europa but the Callistans name Ramavad, the "Silver Moon." By this new increment of silvery blue moonlight, Taran and Koja searched the gloomy landscape rushing by underneath their keel, but could discern no surface feature of importance. They were flying over level plains of scarlet grass, but this came as no surprise to the two adventurers. Shondakor is surrounded on all sides by the grassy prairies of the Haratha Plains, and it was yet too soon to tell in which direction they were flying.

If the *Lankar-jan* were heading west, very soon now they would be able to see the vast jungled tract called the Grand Kumala. But if this did not happen, they could as well be flying north or south or east. If they were headed east, they should be passing over the walls and boulevards and spires of Tharkol the Scarlet City, where Zamara was queen. Koja thought this highly unlikely: that is, he did not believe they would actually *see* Tharkol, even if they were flying in its direction. Privately, he was of the opinion that they would by now already have passed over Tharkol, if they were indeed flying in that direction, but could not have seen it in the darkness.*

Before very long, the firmament flushed with light of a peculiarly beautiful shade of rose-red, which heralded the rising of Ganymede, fourth moon of Jupiter, which the peoples of Callisto call Imavad, the "Red Moon."

By that time, with the varicolored luminance of several moons lighting the dark, it was possible to see the landscape beneath quite clearly.

Taran uttered a short cry, clutched Koja's arm, and pointed ahead of them.

"What is it?" inquired the Yathoon.

"I thought I saw a flash of light—a twinkle!" the boy said breathlessly.

The two watched, straining their eyes, but saw no repetition of the flickering gleam of light that Taran had thought he saw.

Then—

"There it is again!" the boy exclaimed. Then, sorrowfully, "Now it's gone."

Koja said nothing, his chitinous features expressionless, his huge glittering black eyes inscrutable. He

---

* The people of those cities of Thanator known to me are not in the habit of illuminating their cities by night. Watchmen, heralds, or travelers may carry a torch or lantern to see their way, but no method of public illumination is used. Hence it would have been quite easy for Koja and Taran to have flown over Tharkol in the darkness before the Rising of the Moons without realizing it.

stared at the rushing leagues of grassland passing by
beneath them. The light which Taran had glimpsed
might well have been the campfire of a traveler or a
huntsman, or firelight gleaming through the window
of a farmhouse. There was really no way of making
sure . . .

However, Koja thought he knew.

They flew on through the night. After another hour
or so, smaller and dimmer moons began to ascend the
skies. The first to lift above the horizon was a dim red-
gold moon called Kuavad, or Semele, followed before
long by the stark white disc of Daravad, or Leda.

After the Gold Moon and the White Moon had
risen, tiny Antiope and Danae, and the all-but-invis-
ible spark of Taygete climbed into the sky. These are
the outermost of the moons of Jupiter, and lie out
beyond the orbit of Callisto itself, and they are very
much smaller than the giant inner moons, some of
which, like Ganymede or Io or Callisto, are large
enough to be considered small planets.*

Their light was too feeble to visibly augment the
moonlight.

But then the dimness of the moonlit night of Callisto gave way to a ruddy, yellow flush like a dimmer
dawn as the giant bulk of Jupiter floated up over the
horizon, soon occupying nearly a quarter of the sky.
Vast and round, its tawny yellow-orange surface
banded with belts of ruddy ochre, it glared down at

*Captain Dark makes no mention here of the rising of the
ninth moon of Jupiter, Alcmene—either since it is only fourteen
miles in diameter it is simply too small to be visible to the
naked eye from the surface of Callisto, or, since it enjoys a
retrograde orbit to that of the other moons, it rises on the
other side of Callisto. He also fails to remark on the outermost
of the moons, Jove IX, which must be too small to be seen.
Incidentally, the names of these outer moons—Semele, Leda, Antiope, Alcmene, Danae, and Taygete—are not officially recognized. Jove IX has not yet been named anything.

the flying craft with its angry red eye, like some obese and dreadful divinity. It is from the presence of that eye, the Great Red Spot in the southern hemisphere, that the Callistans drew the name Gordrimator—which translates literally as "World of the Red Eye."

By the brilliance of Jove's light, which made the night almost as luminous as day, Koja could see the landscape clearly, and his heart sank within him as he realized that his worst fears were all too well founded.

Ahead of them, directly in the path of their flight, the scarlet meadows were silver-threaded by the meandering paths of twin rivers.

It was the twinkle of momentary reflections of the many moons in the narrow waters of the twin rivers that had made the flashing lights which the keen eyes of Taran had glimpsed.

The boy had never seen the twin rivers before, and looked down at them with surprise and curiosity.

"What *are* they, Koja-*chan*?" he inquired interestedly.

His features unreadable, his voice emotionless and without inflection, Koja explained that they were the Juru-ajand and the Akka-ajand. The boy screwed up his features in puzzlement at this answer, so the Yathoon warrior patiently explained further.

Shondakor is built on the eastern shore of the Ajand, a river that flows north to Soraba and empties into the Corund Laj. But south of the Golden City, the stream divides into twin rivers known to the Thanatorian geographers as the Greater and the Lesser Ajands.

"Then we're flying south, is that it?" inquired Taran.

"Almost precisely southeast, I should say," corrected Koja solemnly.

He did not at that time elaborate on his information. He saw no reason to worry the lad more than he was already worried.

But he could have remarked that the reason why Taran did not recognize this part of Thanator was that the Ku Thad seldom penetrated this region.

For the Ku Thad knew that it was a very dangerous place.

The southlands of Callisto are the dominion of the great nomad Hordes of the Yathoon. These savage warriors exist in perpetual enmity, both with each other and with all of the other inhabitants of Callisto.

The Yathoon nation is divided into five great Hordes or Clans. Nominally, each Horde is independent, and is ruled by its own lord, an *akka-komor,* or high chief. But actually the five Hordes are under the absolute command of the mighty Arkon, who is the sole and only Warlord or Emperor of the Yathoon nation as a whole.

Little is known in cities such as Shondakor or Tharkol or Ganatol of this mysterious and enigmatic personage.

But although Koja had lived for years in Shondakor, he was not a Shondakorian.

He was a Yathoon; and he knew all too well how dangerous and despotic was the cruel and absolute monarch of the Yathoon nation—into whose territories they had inadvertently blundered!

The erratic flight of the *Lankar-jan* continued on. Driven by its whirling rotors and lifted upon the invisible wings of the wind, the little aircraft arrowed on ever deeper into the unknown and unexplored southlands of Callisto.

Aboard, Koja—a renegade self-exiled from his true Clan, and thereby under perpetual sentence of death —and Taran—a Shondakorian youth in the Sky Navy of the Golden City—flew to an unnameable fate.

For each of them, discovery by one of the Yathoon Hordes meant death.

And, with their aircraft out of control, there was nothing they could do about it.

But far behind them, to the northwest, a burly and indefatigeable beast clung doggedly to their trail.

Bozo the *othode* knew that his friends were in danger. And, as long as a spark of vitality remained in his massive body, the faithful Callistan hound would pursue that trail.

Never before had the loyal *othode* followed a trail he could neither sense nor smell. Never, since the very dawn of time, had an *othode* of Callisto attempted to track a flying thing.

But Bozo refused to yield to circumstance, or to permit the novelty of this adventure to faze him.

He would follow the trail of the *Lankar-jan* through the skies into the unknown southland until the last breath left his body and Death itself stole the final atom of strength from his indomitable and courageous heart.

4

Marooned Above the Plain

Neither Koja or Taran got any sleep that night. For that matter, neither did Fido.

The *othode* pup was cold and miserable and hungry. Long before this unseemly hour he would have dined ravenously from a bowl of ground meat mixed with warm milk and crept into his bed of straw in the palace stables to curl up cozily by the warm and breathing bulk of his mighty sire, Bozo.

None of these pleasurable events, to which Fido was comfortably accustomed, had occurred. And, while Fido did not know for certain, he sensed dimly that he had done something to twist awry the normal sequence of events. He crouched miserably on the floor of the cockpit, whimpering plaintively to himself, the nap of his purple fur roughed by the cold winds of this altitude.

He was *very* uncomfortable. And in his heart of hearts the son of Bozo resolved never—*never*—to mess around with flying ships again, if he could possibly avoid it.

Koja and Taran were cold and miserable and hungry. The boy was less cold than he might have been at this height, for the Sky Navy had taken into consideration such hazards of flight when they had designed the uniform issued to sky cadets. His tight blue trousers were snug and warm, his tunic was made of heavy cloth, and his silvered sky-boots were lined with the Callistan equivalent of fleece. And his cape, although rather short, was woven of warm blue wool.

Nor did Koja suffer particularly from the cold. His chitinous armor was proof against the chill winds of this height, and the unique circulatory system of his arthropod anatomy protected him as well.

But they were both hungry, and there was nothing that either of them could do about *that*.

With dawn, everything looked brighter. Koja could see well enough by the light of day to climb back into the tail assembly and disengage the engine, which had a set of alternate controls designed for manual use.

This reduced their airspeed, although nothing much could be done about the height at which they flew. True, standcocks were affixed to both of the pontoons and a quantity of the levitating gas wherewith the pontoons were charged could be bled off. However, once the hydrogen-like gas had been discharged into the atmosphere, it could not be replaced. And the aileron and rudder controls, and those which governed the pitch and tune of the rotor blades, by whose combined means the little gig could have been brought down to the surface, were out of operation.

They were soaring over the southernmost extremities of the Great Plains of Haratha, and seemed to be heading almost exactly southeast. If they continued in this direction they would fly over the Black Mountains, which Koja knew to be infested by the Yathoon Hordesmen. Eventually, he also knew, they would approach the regions of the South Pole. Little was known about the polar regions, save that they were clad in snow and ice.

Were they to continue on their present course until they reached the polar regions, snow crystals would accumulate on the aircraft, forming ice, which would drag the ornithopter down to a disastrous collision with the frozen plains. Either that—a swift, terrible death in the crash—or a slower, more agonizing, indefinitely prolonged death awaited them, as they froze to death by gradual but inexorable degrees.

Neither prospect sounded very inviting.

Koja kept these grim ruminations to himself rather than trouble the boy with them. But he knew that their only real hope lay in bringing the *Lankar-jan* down to a safe landing now—or somehow manage to turn it around. In regard to this second possibility, it seemed all but impossible: the steering mechanism was hopelessly disarranged. And the ship could not be steered manually, by any conceivable manipulation of the ailerons or the tailfin rudder.

If at all possible, he meant to land safely before they reached the Black Mountains. If they were to crack up among the southern peaks, there would be no way to elude capture by the warriors of the savage Horde.

Koja knew all too well the secret that had lain hidden among those grim and ominous peaks for immeasurable ages. He knew also with what fierce tenacity, with what alert and tireless vigilance, the Yathoon warriors guarded all modes of access to those mountains, wherein reposed the ultimate secret of their race, and that portion of the surface of Thanator they deemed most sacred.

By mid-morning the forward velocity of the *Lankar-jan* unaccountably slowed to a mere fraction of its former speed. This unexpected respite cheered Koja immensely, as the reduction in their speed delayed the fateful hour when they would reach the frowning ramparts of the mountain wall and gave him more time in which to accomplish the required miracle of somehow bringing the aircraft down in one piece.

It was Taran who explained the new slowness of their flight. With the engine shut off, the vessel continued to accelerate through momentum alone, somewhat boosted by the strong tailwinds they had experienced all night. The friction of the atmosphere sufficed to retard the velocity of the ornithopter, and the winds had died to a gentle breeze.

Perhaps I should clear up one point here that may be puzzling. While the great flying ships of the Sky Pirates of Zanadar, and their recent offspring, the aerial galleons of the Sky Navy of the Three Cities, are true ornithopters, the little scoutcraft, such as Taran's gig, were not; but I am so accustomed to the employment of this term that I find it difficult to continuously monitor my pen.

An ornithopter, in fact, is a flying vessel that navigates the firmament on the same motive power as that which enables a bird to fly: that is, by flapping its wings. On the ships of the Sky Navy, hinged and jointed vans, manipulated by an ingenious contrivance of wheels and cables, accomplish this action. But the mechanism is far too cumbersome and complicated to be used on the smaller gigs and scoutcraft. They have wings, of course, for stability in flight and maneuverability, but these are fixed and rigid.

The true ornithopter is one of the most interesting inventions of the human imagination. Leonardo da Vinci sketched plans for them in his secret notebooks, but it was reserved for an unknown, unsung genius of Zanadar to create them in actuality, and even then they were only made possible by the fortuitous discovery of a natural gas akin to helium or hydrogen, found among the White Mountains of the northern hemisphere of Callisto.

* * *

By noon the wind had died completely, and the
Lankar-jan drifted alone in the heavens, making no
particular progress in any direction, but coming no
closer to the surface of Thanator.

As I have already mentioned, Koja could have
"bled" some of the levitating gas from the twin pontoons by merely unscrewing the standcocks for a time.
He was not yet prepared to do this because the gas,
once released into the atmosphere, could not be replaced. And the scoutcraft, with its flying abilities
left unimpaired, was their only real hope of returning
to Shondakor with any swiftness or safety.

To attempt the long journey north on foot would
mean traveling overland through Yathoon country,
which was perilous in the extreme. It would also mean
a lengthy and fatiguing journey of many *korads.**
It seemed foolish to disable their craft, thereby making it an absolute necessity that they walk back to
Shondakor, and Koja was determined not to do this
unless all else proved hopeless.

For the moment, then, they were reprieved.

But they were still marooned in the sky.

Taran, filled with the ebullience of youth, was
considerably more optimistic about their chances than
was Koja. He pointed out that they could very well
be rescued at any time now.

" 'Cause last night folks must have noticed that we
weren't there," the boy chirped. "Fido, too! Also, my

---

* The *korad* is the basic unit of land measurement employed
on Thanator, as we of Earth use miles, kilometers, or leagues.
It represents a fraction of the distance from pole to pole, and
according to the Thanatorian reckoning, the Jungle Moon
measures exactly 621.5 *korads* from pole to pole, that number
having some unexplained occult or mystical significance to them.
If the moon Callisto is 4,351 miles from pole to pole, as Captain
Dark agrees it is, then one *korad* is equivalent to about seven
miles.

captain will have seen the berth roster by this morning, an' he'll know I didn't get the *Lankar-jan* back to the docks like I was s'posed to. He'll *know* something's wrong! And then they'll just come looking for us . . ."

Koja made a noncommittal reply; privately he felt events would not progress quite as simply as that. The palace was a huge place with many courtiers, visitors, and officials, and it was easily possible to go days without running into Valkar or Ergon or Tomar and Ylana, or without anyone thinking something might be wrong because you *didn't* see them.

In time, of course, Koja knew quite well that he would be missed, and that eventually his friends would become worried and then alarmed over his prolonged and unexplained absence. And the same was true of Taran—sky cadets cannot just vanish into nowhere without their officers noticing the fact.

But cadets do occasionally take off and go on the Shondakorian equivalent of A.W.O.L., he knew, for boys will be boys even on Callisto. *And there was absolutely no reason for anyone to connect Koja, Taran, and Fido!* Three separate disappearances were no more remarkable than one, and even if a search for the missing three was to be launched, no one could guess where they were or in which direction they had gone. Koja estimated that they had come at least one hundred *korads* from Shondakor aboard the runaway scoutcraft by this time. They had flown for about ten hours, he assumed, before the engine was shut off and the tailwind died, leaving them adrift. That meant that their average velocity had been about seventy miles an hour, which was really better than could have been expected, since the gig's motor was still a fairly primitive device not able to maintain great speed for long.

No one would reasonably expect them to have come so far, even by aircraft.

And to search an area on the surface of the Jungle Moon for one hundred *korads* in every direction, with Shondakor as their starting point, meant there were an awful lot of square *korads* that must be combed to find them.

Such a search, even a concerted one with many parties out, would consume days, probably weeks. And, again, Koja reminded himself of that dire fact— *no one could reasonably expect them to have come this far*.

It looked quite hopeless.

Daylight had warmed the air and they no longer suffered from the cold winds, but they were by now very hungry, having missed dinner, breakfast, and lunch, and would soon become hungrier, with no prospect of another meal in sight.

And there was, of course, another problem becoming ever more evident and that was created by their need to relieve themselves.

Characters in fiction seldom seem concerned about the need to eliminate bodily waste. But this is not a novel, and in real life it is a necessity with which we all must cope. And Koja, Taran, and Fido were increasingly reminded of this necessity as the day wore on.

Especially Fido.

As the day waned into afternoon, a dark clump of trees appeared amidst the endless scarlet meadows.

The Great Plains are not entirely flat and smooth, of course, and are dotted at infrequent intervals with small forests or stands of trees. As this particular clump became clearer to see, since the gentle currents of the air sluggishly propelled the *Lankar-jan* in its direction, Koja and Taran were able to make out that the forest was composed largely of *borath*.

And this gave Koja the idea he was looking for.

The most common tree that grows on the Jungle

Moon is the *jaruka,* with a ropy and twisted black trunk and heavy growth of scarlet foliage. Most of the trees in the Grand Kumala are *jaruka.*

Quite rare, and held in a peculiar form of superstitious reverence by the more primitive denizens of Thanator, is the *sorad* tree. This curious botanical specimen unaccountably reverses the normal coloration and has a scarlet trunk and silky black foliage.

Both *jaruka* and *sorad* are rather small trees, with thick trunks and low, spreading branches.

But the *borath* is something else, in that it resembles our mountain pine or spruce and grows to a considerable height. Indeed, so tall and straight do the *borath* trees grow that I have often thought of them as the sequoias of Callisto.

And the small forest in which direction they were drifting was a stand of *borath* trees.

"Whatever are you doing, Koja-*chan?*" demanded Taran puzzledly—for the gaunt arthropod had climbed out of the cockpit and now sat straddling the rear fusilage, from which point he could untie the mooring cable.

Koja made no reply. As Taran and Fido watched uncomprehendingly, the Yathoon reeled in the long, light cable, measuring its length and calculating the height of the *Lankar-jan* in relationship to the height of the tallest of the *borath* trees which they were slowly approaching.

Then he turned to Taran and expressionlessly commanded the boy to take off his clothes, beginning with his cloak; somewhat bewilderedly, Taran did as he had been told and handed the garment to the arthropod, who proceeded to tear the cape into long strips which he knotted together.

After that, Koja requested the removal of Taran's tunic and, finally, of the close-fitting blue pants which all but completed his Sky Navy uniform.

The boy was left with a brief white loincloth only,

and was afraid that Koja would ask for that next. Save for breechclout, and of course his boots, the youth was naked.

However, he soon perceived the direction of Koja's thought. His garments, torn into strips and knotted together, served to greatly lengthen the mooring cable, to one end of which the collapsible metal grappling hook was fastened. By means of this "sky-anchor" Koja hoped to snag one of the uppermost branches of the tall *borath* trees when they drifted over them.

He hoped, in fact, to anchor the floating craft to the treetops and then either haul the *Lankar-jan* in, hand over hand, or perhaps clamber down the line and descend the tree.

Although he was nearly naked and shivering in the cool breeze, Taran hugged himself excitedly at the prospect of getting down to the ground again and relieving himself behind the nearest bush, and perhaps even finding something to eat.

Then, of course, it began to rain and he was no longer quite so happy.

5

To the Rescue!

More or less as Koja had assumed, his absence from the palace was not at once noted; nor were the disappearances of Bozo and Fido any immediate cause of concern to the court.

The two *othodes* came and went as they pleased, and we were accustomed to their being away for a day or two at a time. Bozo, in fact, was in the process of teaching his ungainly pup how to hunt, and frequently led him into the edges of the Grand Kumala for further lessons in the tracking and killing of game.

As for Koja, the gaunt, solemn arthropod was on good terms with everyone, but his dearest and closest friends were Lukor the Ganatolian, young Taran, my mate Darloona, and myself. From time to time moodiness overcame my insectoid friend, or perhaps he became lonesome for his home on the measureless plains among the mighty Hordes of his kind. On such occasions he might ride out of Shondakor to prowl the grasslands for a day or more, hunting for food, eating his kill, brooding over his somber and forever unknowable thoughts.

This being the way things were, when Koja did not show up for the state dinner in honor of a friendly monarch, our neighbor, Kaamurath of Soraba, nobody thought anything of it. And, when young Taran failed to report to his barracks for bed-check, nobody thought too much of that, either. Young blood is often hot, and the girls of Shondakor were very lovely. It was only when the duty officer, a young *komor* named Jorad, compared rosters and discovered that the scoutcraft *Lankar-jan* had not been checked back into its berth in the dockyards that he began to feel that all might not be well with one of his charges.

Yet, he did not become worried. The nights were summery and the moonlight was very romantic. And, as I have mentioned, the girls of Shondakor are quite beautiful. Taran would not have been the first young sky cadet to take a susceptible young lady for a joyride over the moonlit plains in his skycraft— even though such misbehavior with government property was officially frowned upon.

Jorad himself was only a few years older than Taran, and had a natural tendency to overlook such small, very human infractions of the rules.

But, by the next day, when neither Taran nor the *Lankar-jan* had returned, he became alarmed. Superiors were reluctantly informed and questions were asked in Taran's barracks. None of his fellow cadets could shed any illumination on the mystery, and his best friend, a cadet named Nadan, volunteered that to the best of his knowledge his bunk-mate had no current sweetheart.

Since Taran was an orphan and a ward of the Throne, I, Jandar, was the concerned party who must be informed. Thus, on the evening of the day after his disappearance, a very uncomfortable and heavily perspiring Captain Harad, commanding officer of the cadet legion, came before me in my study to report that the boy was missing.

As it happened, no court balls, banquets, or ceremonies were scheduled for that evening, and my Princess and I had looked forward to spending a cozy and intimate evening together—a pleasure that monarchs find increasingly rare with the weight of empires.

"Perhaps the boy has a sweetheart in town," Darloona suggested with a warm, maternal smile, "and merely let time get away, as can so easily happen with young lovers."

"Such, my Princess, is not believed to be the case," Captain Harad said seriously.

"A joyride, then?" I suggested. "Rather than return his ship immediately after the parade formation, Taran might have felt like taking a little spin—"

"For a full night and a day?" murmured Darloona, with just the slightest frown of worriment beginning to form a crease between her flawless brows. We were both very fond of little young Taran, and thought of him almost as a son—our own son being happily yet too young for such high-jinks as adolescents so easily get themselves into.

"You are right, my beloved." I nodded thoughtfully, beginning to feel the first stirrings of trepidation myself. "The boy must have had an accident—"

"Have I my Prince's permission to organize an aerial search?" the officer asked formally. I told him to launch one immediately: if Taran had carelessly flown beyond the city and had a crack-up, the boy might be injured and in imminent peril.

Later that evening I mentioned Taran's absence to Lukor, as the gallant old sword-master had inquired into the reasons for my distracted mood.

"The lad's missing, eh?" he mused, tugging at his small, neat, silvery beard. "Odd coincidence, my boy— very odd! Because our old friend Koja is away from home, too. Or he was after dinner when I went to his apartments hoping to share a game of Darza * and a

* A boardgame similar to chess and very popular with the Thanatorians.

jug of fine vintage *quarra* with our solemn friend. His servants informed me that their master had not been seen since yesterday afternoon."

"But Koja often gets moody and rides out on the plains to think his own thoughts and commune with nature," Valkar pointed out.

"Not this time, it would seem," fretted Lukor, visibly agitated. "His favorite *thaptor* is still in the stables, because the same possibility also occurred to me, and I bothered to inquire."

I dispatched a page to the dockyards to pass this information along to the searchers, as now it began to seem likely that Koja and Taran, wherever they were, were together.

It was not until the next day, however, that we realized both Fido and Bozo were also missing from the palace. My equerry questioned the guards, at length eliciting the information that Bozo had been seen leaving by a certain gate.

"And Fido was with him?" I asked.

"No, sire, the *othode* was alone," my officer replied.

"Odd," mused Darloona. "Father and son are always together, and Bozo would not have gone hunting alone."

"He left the city and went out into the plains, you say?" I repeated. "And when last seen, was heading southeast? Why in *that* direction, I wonder? If he was going hunting, he would have gone due west, into the Kumala . . ."

"I really do not know, sire," the officer replied. "But the guard said that he seemed to be in a dreadful hurry."

"Mystery upon mystery!" grouched Lukor, scratching the roots of his beard. "I do not like this one bit, my boy! Something is very definitely wrong here."

"I begin to think you may be right, Lukor," I said grimly. And when the search squadron returned on the afternoon of the day following, having combed the landscape between Shondakor and the Kumala, and a similar distance in all other directions, without finding the slightest trace of the scoutcraft or the two *othodes* or Taran and Koja, we all became very definitely fearful for their safety.

"Call out the palace squadron," I commanded. "And have my private yacht made ready for immediate departure."

"Then you're going out searching yourself, eh, lad?" crowed Lukor with gusto.

"I am, indeed. First we shall traverse the Great Plains in the direction Bozo was last seen running," I said grimly. "The stout-hearted old fellow was very attached to Taran, and would lay down his life to protect the boy. If any creature on Callisto knows where Taran has gotten to, I'll lay my money on Bozo the *othode*."

"May I lend my sword to this worthy endeavor?" Lukor cried, jumping up. I smiled.

"There is no sword in all this world I would rather have at back in an adventure," I said truthfully.

A little late, perhaps, but we were off to the rescue at last!

Bozo maintained a steady, tireless stride all that first night. The six bowlegs of the *othode* were short and fat, making him resemble, in that aspect of his person, at least, an English bulldog. But they were strong and powerful, those legs, and did not easily tire. He soon adopted an easy, loping stride that he could maintain without faltering for many hours and that remorselessly devoured the miles.

South of the city, the Ajand River divided into its twin branches, and Bozo followed the southerly curve of the dual waterway as long as its twists and turns did not cause him to turn aside from the direction he pursued with unswerving purpose.

When at length, however, the twists of the river

did impede his path, Bozo did not pause or falter,
but plunged into the waters of the stream and paddled
across to the farther bank. *Othodes* are not used to
swimming much, but, like men, find themselves capable of extraordinary feats when their need is over-
powering.

Emerging at length on the far side of the river, the
devoted Callistan hound dragged himself ashore in
the reeds, wading through reeking alluvial mud, at
last gaining the dry ground. Then he shook himself
dry from head to tail (or to where his tail would
have been, if he'd had a tail). This action was
uncannily like a Terran dog attempting to dry himself
off, yet furthering the canine resemblance.

Once dry, he again took up pursuit.

By midnight he was far to the south of the city,
and growing very weary. Although his iron strength
and endurance were by no means exhausted as yet,
his stamina was not inexhaustible and soon he knew
he must rest. As well, thirst was beginning to torment
him: hunger he could for a time ignore, but his
tongue lolled from his panting mouth and he yearned
for water.

An hour or two before dawn, the need for water
had become a nagging torture to the tireless *othode*.
For the interval he abandoned his quest, and, laying
his nose to the scarlet grasses he began to employ his
sensitive nostrils, hoping to locate a lake or pond, or
perhaps one of the peculiar "mobile oasises" that
are utterly unique to the grasslands of Thanator.

I refer, of course, to the jinko trees. As I have already described this amazing species of perambulating
vegetable in the fourth of these memoirs,* I shall not

---

* See *Mad Empress of Callisto*, Chapter 14. A botanist friend of
mine who has read these books with considerable pleasure, com-
plains the jinko tree is a scientific absurdity. No form of vege-
tation, he argues, possesses more than a rudimentary sensory

bother to discuss the famous "walking trees" of Callisto in any further detail here. Suffice it to say that, ere long, Bozo detected the faint but unmistakable spoor of a good-sized jinko and hunted it down, finally cornering the unhappy vegetable in a cul-de-sac formed by low, rocky hills. While the poor tree trembled in every limb and feebly attempted to jerk its bladder-laden branches up out of his reach, the inexorable *othode* seized in his jaws one fat bladder-leaf, which he detached from its quivering branch with a sidewise wrench of his powerful jaws.

Bozo then proceeded to chew through one end of the distended leaf and lapped up the cool, pure water contained therein, paying no attention to the panicky jinko's attempts to sidle past him and make an escape.

It required the contents of three leaves before Bozo the *othode* had quenched his mighty thirst and was content to rest, panting, permitting the nervous tree to scamper off to a place of safety across the plain.

Returning to his path and taking up the quest again, Bozo was a second time diverted from his goal, however briefly, when a herd of *vanth* galloped across his way. He chased down and killed one of the does and satisfied his hunger by gorging mightily on the raw, bloody meat. Then, after a brief rest, feeling very nearly restored, he continued across the plain.

What Bozo was striving to accomplish with all the tireless devotion of his brave heart was, in fact, an almost impossible task. Had his friends been carried off by riders or wild beasts, he could perhaps have followed their trail for scores of leagues.

---

apparatus and merely vestigial abilities of movement. I pointed out to him that his botanical knowledge was perforce limited to an acquaintance with the life forms of the biosphere of this Earth, and that the same rules might not apply to the fifth moon of Jupiter, whereupon he subsided lamely into silence.

But a flying machine leaves no spoor that can be
followed, even by an *othode* such as Bozo.

All he *could* do, actually, was follow the direction in which the *Lankar-jan* had originally flown.
And this he did with unswerving and unfaltering
accuracy. For some reason, Nature has seen fit to equip
the beasts of Thanator with an innate sense of direction which I, for one, find uncannily accurate.

The people of Thanator share this invaluable trait,
which is particularly strong among the more primitive
inhabitants of the Jungle Moon, such as the Yathoon
barbarians.

All that day the *othode* continued on into the
southeast, on the trail of the runaway scoutcraft.
Twice more he paused to devour a kill, to drink, and
to rest. He saw no slightest sign of civilization during
his progress across the Great Plains of Haratha.

By nightfall he found himself very deeply into the
south. Bozo had no way of knowing how far he had
come in a day and a night, for his kind do not measure
the distances they traverse in miles or kilometers or
korads, but by their expenditures of strength.

And Bozo was approaching the end of his tireless
stores of energy. Still the *othode* did not turn aside
to rest, but doggedly continued the pursuit of those
he loved. By now foam beaded his grinning lipless
gash of a mouth and gathered at its corners and
dripped down to splatter his flanks. From time to time
he stumbled, losing the complicated rhythm of his
six-legged stride.

Once he fell and lay there panting for a time before
grimly lurching to his feet again.

That second night seemed endless. Many times he
fell, but each time he struggled gamely to regain his
feet and continued pursuit. And now his head lolled
and hung low, as if the *othode* no longer possessed
the strength to hold it up. From time to time scarlet

blood flecked the yellowish foam that now slavered continually from his panting mouth.

It was love that goaded Bozo on. The ugly, purple, goggle-eyed creature, with his six bowed legs and grinning, froglike mouth, bore but scant resemblance to an earthly dog, but his heart was a dog's heart, a bottomless well of loyalty and devotion. The love in that heart was inexhaustible, though he was near the end of his body's strength.

Only the inexorable terminus of death could quench the vigor of that mighty heart.

BOOK TWO

KOJA
THE RENEGADE

6

Consequences of a Shower

For some inexplicable reason, it very seldom rains on Callisto.

When, however, it *does* rain on the Jungle Moon, the precipitation makes up in intensity for what it may lack in its frequency. The word "deluge" comes aptly to mind on these occasions.

Busily intent on their approach to the copse of soaring *borath* trees, neither Koja nor Taran had noticed the swift and sudden darkening of the golden skies above them, as moist vapors gathered into storm clouds.

The first they knew of the sudden change in the weather was when they were unexpectedly sluiced from head to foot with icy water. And in no time at all, the naked boy was not only soaked to the skin but chilled to the bone to boot.

Koja did not enjoy being caught in the rain, but it made little difference to him. The chitinous armor wherewith Nature had clad his body made it unnecessary for him to wear any clothing at all (which is why only Taran's clothes were shredded to make an extension on the mooring line, and not Koja's too, in case you had wondered). Hence he had no cloth-

ing for the shower to soak through; the chitinous shell
kept him from suffering any chill or discomfort from
the drenching icy rains.

Fido, however, felt the cold wet intensely, and
raised a sobbing, mournful howl to tell the world
how miserable he was.

They were nearly directly above the tall trees by
this time, so Koja played out his line to its last inch.

Taran sat hugging himself, his teeth chattering and
his knees knocking wetly together, wondering if his
ears were turning blue. As Koja played out the line,
however, he peered over the side—and gasped, and bit
his lip.

It didn't reach.

Koja said nothing, as was his wont. And he didn't
bite his lip, but only because Nature had failed to
equip his kind with lips.

The makeshift line was too short by at least twenty
feet.

Taran groaned and began fumbling with numb wet
fingers at his waist. He was trying to unfasten the knot
that held his loincloth on, but Koja stopped him
with a gesture.

"There is no need for that, my young friend," said
the Yathoon somberly. "Even were we to tear your
clout into the very thinnest of strips, the grappling
hook still would not reach the topmost branches . . ."

Taran was grateful for that much, at least. Wet
through and too thin anyway, the loincloth, though
it served to protect his modesty, afforded no real protection against the inclement weather.

Now Koja clambered out of the cockpit onto the
portside pontoon. The laminated paper wherefrom
the pontoon was constructed was slick with running
water and slippery underfoot. A fall from this height
would kill him instantly.

He lay face down on the pontoon and extended his
arms beneath it, letting the mooring cable dangle

to the greatest possible length, taking advantage of every inch.

It still didn't quite reach.

If the Thanatorians were given to the worship of gods, Koja would have prayed to them then and there, or anyway he would have taken their names in vain by cursing; they were going to drift past the copse in another few minutes, and there their last chance of coming safely down would be lost.

Then he heard a splashing above him, and, craning his featureless casque of a head around, he peered up over his shoulder to see what Taran was doing to make such a sound.

The boy was scooping water out of the cockpit in his hands, as you might bail out a lifeboat in a storm. For, obviously, so intense had the downpour become, the cockpit was rapidly filling up with rainwater.

Swiftly, the Yathoon turned to stare down again through the seething sheets of rain. Was it his imagination, or did the grappling hook now just barely brush against the uppermost leaves? And wasn't the *Lankar-jan* riding just a trifle lower in the air than it had been up to now?

"Taran! Stop bailing out the water!" he clacked sternly in his cold, metallic tones.

"B-but, K-koja-*ch-chan!*" the boy complained through chattering teeth, "It's nearly up to my knees in h-here—!"

"Do not remove so much as another drop of water if you can help it," commanded Koja urgently. "Let the cockpit fill to the brim with rainwater, if it can. Hold Fido's head up, if necessary—*the water we are taking aboard is weighing the skycraft down*—another few inches and we shall be low enough in the air to permit me to snag one of the upper branches with the hook!"

* * *

Inch by inch, the sluggish, wallowing craft sunk nearer to the crest of the tallest *borath* tree. Very little wind was blowing; so thick and heavy fell the deluge that the scoutcraft hovered almost stationary in the sky above the little wood.

The rain was slackening now as the storm clouds drifted slowly over the plains.

But, in time, the unexpected and sudden shower paid off in highly beneficial terms.

Slowly—carefully—with infinite patience, Koja at last succeeded in snagging the topmost branch of the tree. He tugged on the line once it was secure, causing the sharp metal hooks to dig deeply, until they had a firm grip on the soft, flaky bark.

Then—and only then—their perils ended for a time, the three adventurers could relax.

Koja drew the ship down, hauling it hand-over-hand, taking in the slack of the mooring cable, until he was able to draw the *Lankar-jan* down to one of the larger branches, to which he doubly secured the craft.

Getting down from the tree presented a whole new set of problems, of course. *Borath* trees mostly grow their branches at the top and have smooth, straight trunks like the wooden masts of old sailing ships, which means they are not easy to climb down from.

But at last they managed it, taking the job in slow and easy stages. They fashioned a crude sling out of Taran's loincloth, and lowered Fido (who complained vociferously every inch of the way) to the ground by this means; since the awkward *othode* pup could hardly have been expected to climb down voluntarily.

Once he reached the ground, Fido wriggled out of the improvised sling and shook the water from his fur vigorously. The first thing the pup did upon reaching the relative safety of terra firma (or is it *callista firma?*) was to waddle over to the tree, hoist the last two of his three left legs into the air, and salute the tree trunk in the fashion of dogs everywhere.

By the time that Koja and Taran got down to the ground the clouds had rolled away to reveal harsh summer light shining through the tall trees in fierce golden beams. Rather than climb gingerly back into his sopping-wet loincloth, which anyway was now rather strongly redolent of very wet *othode,* the lad simply stretched out naked in the daylight and let the warm radiance dry his skin and bake the chill dampness out of his bones.

Koja let the daylight dry his body, too, but he prowled around, poking through trees and bushes, searching the dead leaves on the ground, and testing vines as if looking for something. Taran wondered vaguely what he was doing, but the boy was exhausted by their long ordeal, and his knees were scraped raw and his leg muscles ached from the difficulty of climbing down the tree, so he was perfectly content to just lie on his back in the damp grass and doze a little in the warm daylight.

After some little time, Koja returned, his gaunt and bony arms filled with ripe fruits, edible nuts, and indescribably delicious green and purple berries— which were the objects of his search.

Fruits and nuts are a sorry substitute for a sizzling steak and a frosty beaker of foaming golden wine, but Taran soon discovered the first great truth of survival in the wilderness: when you are really hungry, almost anything edible tastes good.

His skin and hair dry, his body warm, and his stomach more or less full, Taran felt renewed. He got up, pulled his boots on, even though they were still a bit soggy, and wriggled back into his loincloth. It felt rather clammy next to his skin, but just getting dressed made him feel more like himself.

The three adventurers then compared notes and summed up the total of their resources:

1. One waterlogged but presumably skyworthy scoutcraft, which could be turned about and flown back to Shondakor if its broken control cables were repaired;
2. Two swords in decent condition, although without baldrics, the baldrics having been sacrificed to help extend the mooring cable;
3. Two healthy warriors, even if one of them was only a boy, both presumably able to give a good account of themselves in battle against man or beast;
4. One *othode*.

Thus baldly summed up, the total of their resources was not exactly a figure calculated to give them any particular confidence in their abilities to survive for long in the wild. Hence the quicker they made the flight back to Shondakor the better.

The afternoon had worn on by this point, and nightfall was perhaps an hour away, or a little later. Nevertheless, Taran and Koja hauled themselves back up into the treetops again, and, lying flat on his back against the branch to which the *Lankar-jan* was securely tethered, the young sky cadet made his repairs as best he could.

It wasn't too difficult, actually. The control cables were nothing more than lengths of thin, tough cord which connected the foot pedals to the tailfin rudder and the ailerons on the edges of the wings. When the clumsy Fido had trod too heavily on the pedals he had dislodged them at that end. All Taran had to do, actually, was stretch them tight and tie them back onto the pedals again.

One of them, however, had broken in the middle. This one the boy had to pull together and fasten with a knot. Unfortunately, it was one of the ones that worked the tailfin rudder, and being knotted pulled it more taut than it should have been, which meant the rudder would be stiff and troublesome to work during their return flight to Shondakor. However, this was only a minor problem.

When the repairs were finished, Koja helped Taran get the water out of their airship by the simple expedient of turning the craft over so that the bilge, as it were, was dumped out. The pontoons were still airtight, and the craft itself, as far as they could see, was perfectly airworthy. Even the engine worked, having taken no harm from the rainstorm.

When they clambered down to the ground again so as to fetch Fido, they found an unexpected welcome.

Obviously, the *othode* was not quite as much of a liability on this adventure as they had erroneously assumed when they had compiled that list of resources I have quoted above. For while they had been aloft, working on the aircraft, the ungainly and stumble-footed pup had gone hunting. They came down out of the tree, therefore, to find one proud pup, grinning from ear to ear, waiting for them—with dinner!

Fido had caught and killed two plump, furry forest beasts which rather resembled an unlikely cross between rabbit and squirrel, and might have resembled either of the two more precisely had it not been for the improbable color of their fur, which happened to be a bright pink.

These were, obviously, the same sort of creatures Bozo himself had caught and killed for Prince Lankar in the Grand Kumala, and which the Earthling referred to as either "squirr-bits" or "rabb-ells." The Thanatorians call such creatures *uggars*.*

---

* The scene to which Jandar here refers may be found on page 56 of *Lankar of Callisto*, the sixth volume of these adventures.

Fido was so pleased at his contribution that Taran ran over and hugged the grinning pup, who licked his face with a slurping tongue. Both he and Koja were hungry again, since berries and nuts are a pretty feeble excuse for nutriment for busy, hard-working adventurers, and the very thought of hot broiled *uggar* meat made their mouths water.

And they could, of course, depart for the return flight to Shondakor the Golden a wee bit later than they had planned.

So while Taran scrabbled about gathering dry twigs and leaves and moss for a cook-fire, Koja returned yet again to the treetop and came back down with the tinderbox wherewith a thoughtful and foresighted supply officer had decided each scoutcraft cabin should be outfitted.

By nightfall the two plump *uggars* were sizzling juicily above a smoky little fire, having been neatly skinned, gutted, and skewered on a sharp twig.

A little later they proved every bit as delicious as Taran and Koja had imagined they would be. The two polished off every last succulent morsel of their dinner, not forgetting to reward Fido with numerous tidbits and gobbets, and all of the less chewable parts.

By this time night had fallen, but not yet had the first of the many moons yet ascended to glimmer red and silver, blue and gold and white in the sky, like paper lanterns.

But it was still light enough for them to see the great black arrow when it clove whistling through the air to sink quivering in the trunk of the *borath* tree as they were about to begin climbing it for the return flight.

They whirled, snatching out their swords, as the first gaunt, stilt-legged warriors of the Yathoon Horde came charging through the brush to seize them.

7

Crimson Steel

Thrusting the boy behind him with one arm, Koja sprang forward to confront the charging warriors. From the baldric slung across his thorax, he drew his whip-sword and stood to face the attack of the unknown foemen.

The clan markings painted across the hard, shiny chitin of their breasts in scarlet, black, and purple were not at once familiar to him. This was odd, because Koja was acquainted with the insignia of each and every Clan in all of the mighty Yathoon Horde, and for there to have existed yet another which he had never heard of was virtually impossible.

But it had been some years now since Koja had last ridden with the Horde; obviously, in the interval, a new tribe or group of tribes had evolved into being. This was a constant factor in the life of the Horde. A disagreement between rival factions in the selection of a new *akka-komor,* or high chief, sometimes may result in the withdrawal of the defeated candidate, together with his followers, their retinues, cadets, servitors, and slaves, from the parent Clan to establish another. This was the case in the present instance,

Koja assumed. But he found himself a bit too busy to
give the matter much thought.

The warriors facing him were fully armed, as if for
war. The Yathoon warriors, covered as they are with
a slick gray armor of tough, flexible chitin like a crab
shell, wear no clothing, save for such utilitarian garments as a war harness or a baldric, or both.

The baldric is a belt of red *yathrib* leather slung
across the upper thorax from shoulder to hip and
extending across the back. By its means the Yathoon
warrior carries his whip-sword scabbarded between the
shoulders (the arthropods, of course, don't really have
"shoulders," merely armored joints, but never mind
about that). This is necessary because of the inordi-
nate length of these weapons, which measure a full
sixty inches from barbed tip to hilt.

The war harness, worn usually only for armed conflict with another Clan, is an affair of belts and
straps worn over the shoulders and fastened twice
about the upper portions of the thorax. From this
several subsidiary weapons or accouterments are suspended by brass or silver rings: a scabbarded dagger
about the size and length of a U.S. Army bayonet, an
ugass; a small, light, throwing-axe about the size of a
Boy Scout's hatchet; and sometimes a blunt-tipped,
thick short-sword called a *zak*. A leather bottle of
water or wine may often be clipped to the harness as
well, as a soldier would carry a canteen. Generally,
they wear an unstrung bow of black wood slung across
the thorax, with a leathern quiver of black or scarlet
arrows hung behind the left shoulder.

The warriors who faced Koja, silent and inscrutable
and, for the moment, immobile, wore both harness
and baldric, fitted out with all of the above equipment
and accouterments. As well, they carried lassos of
braided leather thongs, wound into tight loops and
suspended from a hook on the left side of their har-

nesses, and with the use of these lassos they were uncannily adept, as I had good reason to know.

For a moment this silent confrontation lasted, but
only for a moment and no longer. Then the leader of
the troop—a towering brute with one of his twin
brow-antennae broken off short, lending him an
extraordinarily raffish, devil-may-care appearance—
swiftly reached with his right hand up over his right
shoulder, grasped the pommel of his whip-sword, and
sprang forward, leaning from the hips in fighting
stance, and unlimbering his whip-sword, all at the
same time and in the same easy flow of action.

Koja sprang to meet him, and they engaged their
blades while Taran watched open-mouthed.

The Yathoon whip-sword is a terrible weapon, a
slim, flexible strand of razor-sharp steel, tipped with
a hooked barb whose shape resembles an arrowhead.
The Yathoon fight with these by swinging them in
deadly hissing circles, with which they weave a shim-
mering web of lethal steel before them, like an all-but-
invisible shield. When they strike at each other, they
snap the barbed tip forward and jerk it back, hoping
to rip a jagged furrow across the face or thorax or
abdomen of their adversary—thus slaying or crippling
the foeman with a single stroke.

In open places, this cobralike whipping stroke is
often made from mid-air. With their long, many-
jointed legs, which resemble the hind limbs of the
praying mantis or the terrestrial grasshopper, the
Yathoon are easily capable of incredible leaps into the
air. A Yathoon swordsman can and often does leap
entirely over his foe, striking at his unprotected head
as he springs over it. In this confined space, however,
with tree boughs blocking the sky, such aerial tactics
were difficult or even dangerous. So they fought face
to face, snapping those deadly blades like sharp steel
whips, leaping forward with each stroke and springing

backward immediately after in order to avoid the
counter-stroke.

It was graceful, even beautiful, in a cold, murderous
way—like a ballet—a dance of death.

Koja and his challenger were well matched, of an
identical height (some seven feet), with arms and also
whip-swords of similar length. For a few moments,
they fenced in this deadly dance without results: then
the others, restive or impatient, sprang forward, one
to either side of Koja's opponent, the chieftain with
the broken antenna, whose name later turned out to
be Gothar.

Koja swerved sideways, swift and supple as a striking serpent. His whirling blade struck suddenly to the
left, catching his hapless foe across the face. His eyes
ceased being glittering black jewels and became a
flying splatter of wine-colored jelly. The barbed tip
caught in the corner of the eye socket and cracked the
surface of the warrior's chitin, breaking away a portion of his skull. For a moment Taran caught a brief,
sickening glimpse of the Yathoon's naked brain, a
reddish gray convoluted lump of wet, glistening tissue.

Then the warrior seemed to come apart at the joints
and fell in a jumble of limbs to sprawl on the scarlet
turf. He collapsed as a jointed wooden puppet might
collapse if all of the puppet's strings were severed in
the same instant.

Koja then leaped sideways, avoiding strokes from
the two remaining swordsmen, and, snatching up the
whip-sword his fallen adversary had dropped, he ad-
dressed the twain with a sword in each hand.

Fighting with two swords is a particularly difficult
practice, a matter for precise rhythm. I have seen it
done in my time, but not often: Lukor can do it with
amazing deftness, but I had not realized Koja's own
accomplishment in this specialty.

In less time than it would take me to describe the
scene, Koja had felled the second of his opponents,

and found himself once again engaged with his original foeman, Gothar—he of the crippled antenna. While Koja was otherwise engaged, Gothar had taken advantage of the momentary respite to rest and catch his breath. Now he attacked Koja with redoubled ferocity.

But now Koja was doubly armed! And perhaps Gothar had never before faced a single swordsman who held in each hand a dripping and murderous length of razor-sharp crimson steel . . .

When Gothar fell, clutching at his naked entrails as they oozed from the wide, ragged gash in his abdomen, Koja charged the other warriors who had lurked behind in order to permit their chieftain and the two warriors who were his lieutenants to have the pleasure of the kill.

Here the tree branches grew higher above their heads, and Koja was able to employ one of those incredible leaps into the air that make Kathoon barbarians feared opponents, dreaded by the swordsmen of more civilized parts of Thanator. Bounding over the heads of the first rank, Koja struck down between his bent legs with either sword in swift rhythm—*flick!*—*flick!*—and two more warriors sprawled, spouting crimson on the crimson turf.

When he landed on bent feet again, however, it was to find himself ringed in by foemen. The one who stood, as it chanced, at his back was waiting to strike just as soon as Koja's steel had been engaged by one of the Yathoon in front of him.

When this happened, the warrior at the rear set his blade into a whirl, preparing to take Koja from behind. But, as Fate would have it, he was taken from behind, himself, although he did not at once realize it. The sharp, stabbing pain caught him quite by surprise, and he stared down to see the encrimsoned point of a slim rapier emerging from his vitals. He was still staring at it in blank bewilderment when the strength drained from him and he fell forward into gathering darkness.

Behind him, young Taran withdrew his rapier with a practiced twist of his wrist and whirled to strike at another of the warriors grouped around Koja. The arthropods had taken no notice in particular of the boy, obviously not considering him to be dangerous. The young of their own kind never partake in adult quarrels until they have achieved the Yathoon equivalent of what would in human terms be called puberty, and it is quite a common sight for a male Yathoon's sons to stand idly by while their father fights to the death in a duel or similar engagement. The young Yathoon think nothing of this, being immune to filial sentiment.

Then too, such are the curious customs associated with the manner in which the Yathoon warriors raise their young, the cubs never actually know which warrior might be their own father, so to partake in any adult quarrel would seem unreasonable and pointless to them, even if it were not forbidden by their Horde traditions.

Koja had killed seven of the enemy warriors and little Taran himself had slain another two of them, when one of the sub-lieutenants decided that the strength of numbers might just possibly not be sufficient to subdue these two strangers, and lent Destiny a hand—and rather an "underhand" it was, too.

In a trice this fellow (his name Koja later found out to be Uthak) had whipped out his lasso and tossed it at the fighting stranger. The first thing Koja knew about it was when the leather thong fell about his shoulders and tightened around his upper arms, pinning them to his sides. Then Uthak pulled the lasso taut with a savage jerk which yanked Koja off his feet. He fell to the ground and, before he could strive to free himself, other loops were whipped around his arms and legs. Within moments he was bound hand and foot, and was completely helpless.

Taran, however, was wary as a young wolf, and the Yathoon warriors found they could not snare him from behind as they had Koja, because the boy set his back against a tree and, using the point of his rapier, either flicked aside or cut through each lasso they tossed at him. Finally, they battered his slender blade aside and closed in on him. They beat him into half-consciousness with balled fists and took his weapon from him.

They did not, however, slay either of their captives. When one of them, a warrior called Hoog who had one blinded eye, inquired of Uthak why he was permitting the two to retain possession of their lives, Uthak made a sensible reply.

"Dead men make poor slaves."

"That is so," mused Hoog thoughtfully, savoring the essence of the remark with the manner of one to whom a Great Truth has been given.

"Besides," added Uthak, who seemed to be in charge of the squad, now that Gothar was dead, "this carrion"—he kicked Koja lightly in the side as indication of which particular carrion he referred to—"slew the chieftain Gothar and six other warriors. He is no novice with a sword. If it is the decision of Fanga that he be permitted to continue living until we reach Sargol, then he may afford us some rare entertainment in the Arena."

"That is also true," admitted Hoog slowly. Then—and he would probably have smirked obsequiously if Nature had provided Yathoons with the prerequisites for smirking—he added, "I admire the superior reasoning powers of the *juru-komor* Uthak."

Uthak nodded slightly, as if giving a receipt for the compliment.

Taran, lying there groggily while he was bound, wondered dimly what or where Sargol was.

Koja, who was also conscious, did not wonder about Sargol because he knew what it was. And it was bad news to him that the Clan whose captives they were seemed en route to Sargol, because he knew what happened there. And, anyway, he had other things to occupy his mind.

He was thinking about the Arena.

When his captives were disarmed, thoroughly searched, and had been lightly but securely trussed in such a manner that they could ride, sub-lieutenant Uthak led his band to where their *thaptors* had been tethered just within the borders of the little copse.

None of the Yathoons had bothered to look up above their heads, during or after the fight. But if they *had* looked up, they would probably have seen the scoutcraft moored to the branch above them. That they did not discover the flying vessel, Koja accounted the one small favor Fate had tossed them, as one tosses a bone to a starving dog.

The Yathoons bundled their captives onto the *thaptors* that had belonged to the slain warriors and rode out of the copse. They did not bother to burn or bury the bodies of their fallen comrades; such ways were not Yathoon ways. The Yathoon is not a religious or even a superstitious creature, and therein he differs enormously from other barbarian nations, such as those of the Earth.

Neither is he at all sentimental. A dead body is just a dead body to a Yathoon: something to be looted of any useful or valuable possessions, and then to be simply left where it had fallen.

Having stripped the corpses, then, Uthak's band rode away leaving them to the Callistan equivalent of crows.

Taran and Koja rode with them.

There was no sign of Fido. The *othode* had vanished into the brush at the first sign of the Yathoon squadron, and had still not reappeared.

At least *he* had escaped capture, thought Taran.

8

The Doom of Borak

The *thaptors* were tethered just within the edges of the copse, where they would be out of sight, hidden from discovery by any wandering predators or from the eyes of the hunters or warriors of an enemy Clan. Koja and Taran were assisted to mount the saddles, then tied in place with their hands tied behind them to render impossible any attempt at escape. The reins of their steeds were managed by their captors, who rode stirrup to stirrup on either side of them.

Thaptors are large, partly domesticated wingless birds or befeathered horses, or an unlikely combination of the two. Try to picture swift-footed, four-legged ostriches crossed with Shetland ponies and you will have a mental image of what they look like. They always remind me of the griffins or hippogriffs of legend and myth.

They have curved, parrotlike beaks and mad, round eyes. I call them "partly domesticated" because they have never been completely tamed or broken to the saddle and easily become cantankerous, restive, and uncooperative. Thanatorian riders carry a little dumb-bell-like club called the *olo* which is hung on the saddle-bow, with which to beat their steeds into docility whenever they take it into their heads to ride off in some other direction than that in which their rider wants to go, or attempt to bite a piece out of his leg, or both—which they do quite frequently.

The squadron of warriors that had been under the chieftaincy of Gothar had obviously been a party of hunters out scavenging for game, for the captors of Taran and Koja carried the carcasses of slain beasts lashed over their *thaptors'* backs behind their saddles. This could have meant that the main encampment of the Clan lay some day or two days' ride distant, thought Koja, which greatly increased his and Taran's chances to break free and make their escape, especially since darkness had fallen.

However, such did not prove to be the case.

Within an hour or so, the hunting party entered the Yathoon encampment and rode between rows of tents toward the center of the temporary base. Koja learned about this clan by listening to the desultory conversations between his captors as they rode, and by reading the meanings of the tribal inscriptions painted upon the warriors' bodies, saddles, accouterments, and war shields. The smallest of the six Clans, it was known as the Garukh Clan, and had been formed when the high chief, Fanga, withdrew with his retinue and followers from the great Kandar Clan when that clan had chosen another as high chief instead of Fanga.

The new Clan was quite small, as Koja might have guessed, with many cadets and servitors and slaves but few adult warriors. Bad blood existed between the Kandars and the members of the new Garukh Clan, and they were at open warfare. Any Kandar the Garukhs caught, they killed.

Perhaps I should explain here that the Yathoon barbarians are preliterate. They have no written language of their own and, with very few exceptions, can neither read nor write nor understand the universal written language of Thanator. They do, however, employ a crude and rudimentary form of sign language, a symbolism not at all dissimilar to heraldic blazonry. The trouble with these symbolic drawings is that they more or less mean whatever you want them to mean, and it takes a little getting used to them before you can make them out with any sort of accuracy, since the same symbol may mean six different things to members of each of the six different Clans.

By the time Koja had deduced that he and Taran had been taken prisoner by a chieftain of the Garukh Clan, and that the Garukhs had broken away from the Kandar Clan, with whom they were at war, he began to rejoice grimly in the fact that during his years of residence in Shondakor in the retinue of Prince Jandar he had gotten out of the habit of painting his tribal signs across his thorax.

And he would have begun to sweat, if he could, for Koja had been a chieftain of the Kandars.

It was late at night when Uthak led his hunters into the main encampment of the Garukhs, and too late to display his captives to the *akka-komor,* the high chief of the Clan, since that personage had already retired after a feast at which he had taken aboard a considerable quantity of the thin, sour beer which the Yathoon habitually imbibe in place of the wines or brandies brewed by the more civilized races of the Jungle Moon.

The high chief, Fanga, was as coldly emotionless as were all of his kind, but of a truculence unusual among the Yathoon and given to deadly outbursts of ferocity. Not at all, you will understand, the sort of individual who takes kindly to being awakened in the middle of the night to examine prisoners. Therefore Uthak ordered Koja and Taran chained for the night in the slave pens, together with the various other captives and possessions of the Clan, deciding to report to Fanga on the death of the chieftain Gothar and the capture of a clanless Yathoon renegade and what Uthak considered his human slave, the boy Taran.

Most of the slaves and prisoners were already asleep when Hoog and Uthak brought the two new captives in and chained them to one of the poles sunk in the earthen floor of the pen for precisely that purpose. The chains were attached to their ankles, and while they were being secured to the pole, Koja looked around him keenly in the light of the torch Hoog held, getting a look at the other captives.

He was surprised to see a young human female among the slaves, and he was even more surprised to discover himself being chained next to a stalwart and powerful Yathoon whom he recognized at a glance, although they had not seen each other for many years.

"Jaruga, O Borak," he muttered in low tones, once the warriors had withdrawn and they were left alone. "Many moons have risen and set since last we feasted together at the Games of Sargol. Do you remember Koja, chieftain of the Kandars?"

"Jaruga, O Koja," replied the other, repeating the simple word of greeting commonly used among the members of the Horde. "I remember well how you bested me with the spear during the Games, and how I bested you with the bow. You would be wise to desist from mention of the Kandars here, for so great is the hatred and the jealousy with which the high chief, Fanga, regards all members of your Clan that instant death would be the echo of that Clan's name, were you so foolish as to utter it in the presence of one of his warriors."

"I thank you for the warning," said Koja noncommittally. "But tell me, how come you here, chained like an ordinary slave in Garukh irons, when to my best knowledge you have succeeded to the rank of high chief of your own nation since last we met?"

"Alas, the Haroob Clan now groans under the lash of a traitor and a usurper," said Borak grimly.

"Whilst I, their true leader, have been driven into exile and outlawry by trickery and deceit. The tale, however, is a long and an unhappy one, and is best saved for another time, as dawn is not far off and we must be rested for the morrow."

"Tell me, then, but one thing more," urged Koja. "That human female tethered to the far wall of the tent: who is she, and what is her nation? For she seems royal in dress and demeanor, and her coloring reminds me of a comrade from distant Ganatol."

"The female indeed harks from Ganatol, as I have been given to understand, although we have not had speech together since she was chained amongst us," said Borak. "Her name is Xara, and she is of the royal house of that city, captured by Fanga's scouts while on an official mission of some sort to one of the southern cities; I believe it was Shondakor the Golden."

"Indeed?" muttered Koja, his curiosity aroused. "How long has she been among the slaves of Fanga?"

"Not long: a month, perhaps a bit more. And now let us find what poor rest we can in the harsh chains of captivity," said Borak. And, with those words, he turned on his side and slept.

Koja, however, did not sleep. He was wondering what mission had brought Xara, Princess of Ganatol, into the slavery of the Yathoon Horde.

The following morning the *komad* Uthak made his report to Fanga, who was far from pleased to learn that one Yathoon warrior and a human boy had slain nine of his huntsmen, the chieftain Gothar among them. Koja and Taran were brought before him in chains to be interrogated.

Fanga looked Koja up and down, while Koja observed him in return. The high chief of the Garukhs was a powerful adult arthropod and was evidently a veteran warrior of great prowess, for his chitinous armor bore many scars from ancient wounds gotten in combat or in the *duello*. There was something about the cold, unwinking stare of his glittering eyes that made Koja distrust him, and something in the grim, threatening set of his features that he did not like.

But he did not recognize Fanga, which was one thing to be thankful for. Apparently they had never before met, even in Sargol. That meant that Fanga did not and could not recognise him as a former chieftain of the hated Kandars.

"As a warrior of the Yathoon Horde, you must belong to one Clan or another," observed Fanga heavily. "To which Clan do you owe allegiance?"

"To none," said Koja levelly. And it was no less than the truth he spoke, for he had long ago given up his allegiance to the Kandars to join the retinue of his friend, Jandar of Shondakor.

"Then you are *aharj*?" queried Fanga. The word meant, approximately, one who was an outcast or an outlaw, forever exiled from membership in his native Clan.

Koja twitched his brow-antennae in the Yathoon equivalent of an uncaring shrug. "You have said it," he remarked tonelessly.

The comment could be interpreted as meaning either "so you say," or "you have guessed the truth." Fanga chose the second interpretation, which was fortunate for Koja.

The high chief said nothing, but continued to stare down at Koja from his dais. He was a fearsome figure, was this Fanga, for as if his ghastly scars did not make him hideous enough, he chose to adorn his person with a girdle and a necklace made of grinning skulls —the skulls of humans and of Yathoons. He was grim and terrible, and little Taran shuddered at the look of him.

Then he nodded, absorbing the information, and

did not bother to inquire further into Koja's Clan. The reason for this was, quite simply, that when a Yathoon goes *aharj* he has foresworn all Clan allegiance. In simple fact, then, Koja was no longer a Kandar, and had ceased to be one the very moment he had ridden out of the Kandar encampment, assisting Jandar the Earthling to escape. Therefore, it made no particular difference what Clan Koja had once belonged to: an outlaw was simply that, an outlaw, and fair game.

It never occurred to Fanga that Koja might have been a Kandar. "Uthak says you are a master swordsman," growled Fanga. "Is that true?"

"It is," acknowledged Koja expressionlessly. Being a Yathoon, it was neither in his nature to boast or to affect a modest disclaimer of his prowess. The Yathoon tend in general to be the most honest and straightforward of all of the races of Thanator, for so emotionless are they that they simply tell the absolute and literal truth, ungarnished by flattery, egotism, or modesty. Koja knew his own talent, and he acknowledged it.

"Then we shall not give this *aharj* the swift execution generally afforded to *aharj* warriors when captured," decided Fanga. "We shall save him for the Games."

"And when, O Fanga, do we leave for Sargol?" inquired Uthak, newly raised to full chieftaincy to fill the command position left vacant by the death of Gothar.

"That has yet to be decided," growled Fanga moodily. "But it will be soon enough, I warrant," he added with a cold, gloating look at the impassive figure of Koja. "*Too* soon, for some among us. Take these captives away."

Hoog, who had charge of the captives of Uthak's tribe, set Taran to work grooming the *thaptors*. Koja he chained next to Borak on a work detail, and all that morning they labored together. During infrequent rest periods they found further opportunities to talk a little.

"How was it, Borak, that you came to lose your position among the Haroobs?" Koja asked during one of these brief respites from the day's toil.

In measured tones which reflected absolutely no emotion, Borak related that he had ridden with his Clan into the grasslands that lay about the city of Tharkol about two years earlier. At that time he had been only a *komor* of the Haroobs, merely one of the dozen or so chieftains who led the several Haroob tribes under the command of Tugar, the high chief. Borak had taken several humans prisoner during a hunting expedition, it seems, and when these captives escaped, which was very soon after he captured them, the Clan was thereafter attacked by Shondakorian legions searching for these same lost humans, who were evidently persons of considerable importance in the Golden City of the Ku Thad.

Now, as it happened, Koja had independent verification of this part of Borak's tale—for those people he had taken prisoner two years or so ago had been none other than Ergon and Glypto, Zamara of Tharkol, Darloona, my Princess, and I, Jandar.*

In their escape, the humans had driven away all of the Haroobs' *thaptors* in a stampede staged as a diversion: therefore, when the legions came, the Clan was forced to fight on foot, and suffered enormous losses. Tugar, the high chief, accused Borak of criminal negligence and laxity in guarding his captives so carelessly, and would have had him put to death had not Borak claimed his right to challenge the high chief to personal combat.

This right, called *tharaj*, is a privilege that ac-

---

* See *Mad Empress of Callisto*, Volume Four, for an account of this captivity.

companies the rank of chieftain. Any chieftain may challenge the high chief of his Clan to personal combat at any time, just as any Clan chief may challenge the mighty Arkon or emperor of the whole Yathoon Horde to combat at any time.

Borak told of the battle, which had been a grim and terrible ordeal. After suffering many wounds he had at length slain the high chief and become high chief himself. But in gaining the throne of Tugar, he had incurred the enmity of a rival chieftain named Gorpak, who had never been particularly friendly with him when they had been of equal rank, and who now became his deadly enemy once he had achieved a rank superior to that of the vindictive Gorpak.

Gorpak, it seems, had either bribed or cajoled one of Borak's followers, a natural-born schemer named Hooka, to incriminate Borak in a clever plot. The rivalry between Gorpak and Borak was well known to the warriors and chieftains of the Clan, and when Gorpak fell suspiciously ill of a complaint whose symptoms were similar to those caused by a certain poison called *axad,* and a phial of *axad* was found concealed among Borak's trove of treasures, it was obvious to all that Borak had poisoned Gorpak in order to rid himself of a dissenter.

Of course, Gorpak was only faking his illness, and the phial of *axad* had been placed in Borak's trove by the cunning Hooka.

The crime was an affront to the honor of warriors. Borak was deprived of the rank of high chief and declared *aharj* and driven into exile and outlawry, later taken prisoner by the Garukhs. Thus did Borak become a slave. Gorpak, making a miraculous recovery from his "poisoning," had replaced Borak in the role of high chief.

Koja nodded, saying nothing. It was a cruel tale, and a hard turn of Fate. But life itself is hard and cruel in the wilderness of the Great Plains, where the savage and restless Horde wanders forever, at war with itself and with every other living thing upon the face of Thanator, the Jungle Moon.

9

Xara of Ganatol

Several days after these events, Koja was attached to another work detail and found himself chained next to the handsome young woman named Xara, who Borak the Yathoon had said was a Ganatolian of the royal house. He observed her unobtrusively, discreetly, curious as to her history, yet too diffident to strike up an acquaintance with a female of another species.

The Ganatolians are unique among the races of Thanator in that they most closely resemble the human inhabitants of my native world. Indeed, dress a citizen of Ganatol in human clothing, and you could set him or her down in the streets of Chicago or Seattle or Boston without attracting the slightest attention to his appearance.

This cannot be said, of course, for citizens of the Bright Empire of Perushtar, who are all bald and as red of skin as a ripe tomato. Nor can it be said of my own Shondakorians, who, with their golden skin, crimson hair, and green or amber eyes make a decidedly exotic appearance. Nor can it truly be said of the extinct or scattered races, such as the Sky Pirates of Zanadar or the bandit warriors of the Chac Yuul, whose physical characteristics differed considerably from earthborn humans.

The Ganatolians, in fine, have fair skins, eyes of blue, black, or brown, and sleek dark hair. They look like ordinary Englishmen or Americans, and are among the most highly civilized and cultured of the races of Callisto.

And Xara could only have been a woman of Ganatol. Her skin was as tender and as fair as that of a camellia's petal, and her long thick hair was black as midnight and fine as silk. Her eyes were large, fringed with black lashes, and blue as any sapphire, and her lips were perfectly shaped, ripe, and luscious.

She was, in fact, a remarkably beautiful and desirable young woman. Even Koja, as alien to her kind as any insect might be to a mammal, had mixed with human beings long enough to recognize that she possessed an extraordinary loveliness.

She seemed sad and depressed, but resigned to her fate, saying little to her fellow captives, simply performing whatever tasks were assigned to her with docility and strict obedience. However, she affected not even to notice the presence of Koja at her side, never looked at him or spoke to him, and beyond a slight, disdainful wrinkling-up of her nostrils—as if she smelled something disgusting or repulsive—made not the slightest sign that she was even aware of his existence.

It is true that Koja, like all of his kind, possessed a distinct odor characteristic to the Yathoon. It was a sharp medicinal smell, as back on my native world, Earth, certain insects smell of formic acid. In point of fact, however, Koja's odor was neither disgusting nor particularly disagreeable: in fact, I rather enjoy his smell. And, for Koja's part, he once informed me that, to the senses of a Yathoon, humans also possess a distinct and characteristic odor which he does not find unpleasant.

He decided, however, that for whatever the reason, Xara did not wish to converse with him, and she desired him to leave her alone as much as possible. Some of the people of Thanator regard the Yathoon insectoids as lowly or subhuman forms of life, and even have a name for them—*capoks*. The word does not have complimentary associations.

Despite the unfriendliness Xara of Ganatol displayed toward him, Koja did what he could to make her burdens lighter, even taking upon himself certain of the dirtier tasks given to her by one-eyed Hoog, the slavemaster.

The first few times Koja did this, Xara pretended not to notice, although her curiosity was aroused. One who regards a Yathoon as a barely sentient lower life form does not expect to find them possessing the instincts of a gentleman. For this reason, Xara was intrigued by Koja's protective ways and occasionally studied him intently when she did not think he might notice.

But on the sixth day after they were chained together, Koja deliberately interposed his body between the Ganatolian girl and the punishment of Hoog's lash, and she could no longer ignore his peculiar behavior toward her.

It came about in this wise: they had been toiling together in the galley tent where the Yathoon prepared their food. Xara was weary from the long day's labor and, when instructed to carry a huge platter of food into the adjoining tent where the chieftains ate, her ankle turned, she slipped, and spilled the food onto the ground. Hoog was upon her in a trice. Seizing her wrist, he twisted it cruelly and hurled her upon her face in the filth. But when he unlimbered his whip to beat her, suddenly Koja was there.

"Step aside, while I teach this female not to turn

a feast into so much garbage," growled Hoog, clashing his mandibles.

"It was my fault," said Koja, "for I tripped her and made her drop the tray."

"Your fault, was it?" snarled Hoog, making his whip sing in the air. "Then the punishment is yours as well!"

And while Xara lay there, petrified with astonishment, staring up with wide eyes, Koja stood with bent shoulders, stolidly and uncomplainingly accepting the bitter kiss of the lash that should have been hers. He did not utter a sound, and eventually Hoog wearied of whipping one who neither whimpered nor cowered, and turned away to other business.

The Yathoon are not ordinarily a cruel people, for they seem to lack almost every emotion found in humanity, including the urge to be cruel as well as the impulse to be kind. Hoog, like his master Fanga, was somewhat unique in this respect, that they both seemed to faintly enjoy either inflicting pain upon the helpless or watching it being dealt out.

But they are essentially practical. An injured slave is a slave that can do less than an ordinary day's work. Hence Koja was returned to his quarters so that the wounds caused by the whipping could be treated medically.

"Let me do that," said an unexpected voice from behind Koja as he lay on a cot in order that his wounds might be cleansed. The next moment he felt the soft touch of human hands as they spread a soothing ointment which eased the sting of his cuts— for while the chitin armor is not easily cut, the cartilage which connects the plates of this armor is indeed vulnerable to such injuries.

Turning his head stiffly, he saw that the unguent was being gently applied to his back by none other than Xara of Ganatol.

* .* *

That night they were chained together in the slave
pens, and Koja without thinking arranged Xara's
sleeping-cloths for her.

"Why do you do things for me?" she murmured
perplexedly. "Why did you accept the punishment
that was my due because it was caused by my own
clumsiness? Always I have thought that *capoks* are
immune to kindness and to sentiment, yet you seem
to possess these emotions."

"I have learned gentle ways from gentle masters,"
said Koja. "For I believe that I am the first of my
race to have learned the meaning of the word 'friendship.' And I have learned also that a kindness given
freely is oft repaid a thousand times over. Even a
capok, my Princess, is capable of learning."

The girl from Ganatol flushed scarlet to hear that
word from Koja, and she bit her lip in vexation. A
while later she spoke, in a subdued voice.

"Forgive me for calling you a *capok*, Yathoon."

"I forgive it freely, for the word was spoken in
ignorance," said Koja.

"Have you . . . a name?" she asked shyly. "Mine is
Xara of Ganatol."

"My name is Koja, Princess."

"How do you know that I am a princess . . . Koja?"
the girl murmured.

The Yathoon warrior explained that Borak of the
Haroob Clan had told him something of the circumstances surrounding her capture, and that she was a
daughter of the royal house of Ganatol and had been
en route to Shondakor the Golden when seized by
Fanga's warriors.

"That is true," she sighed. "By now my royal
father will have become convinced of my death, or of
the futility of my mission to Shondakor, or perhaps
of both."

Koja surveyed the despondent girl, his glittering, jeweled eyes expressionless, his armored features inscrutable.

"I, too, desire nothing so much as to reach the Golden City of the Ku Thad, together with my small human friend, the boy Taran," he confessed. "Perhaps we can yet be of assistance to each other in securing our freedom, and together we can find our way to Shondakor. Two heads are better than one, as I have often heard Jandar remark."

She glanced at him, surprised.

"Why should a Yathoon of the Horde seek the city of the Ku Thad? And how came you to be upon such close terms with Prince Jandar—if it is truly he of whom you speak?"

Koja patiently explained that he had long been resident in Shondakor the Golden, and that he was a courtier in the retinue of Prince Jandar, whom he accounted his first and oldest friend. Xara may perhaps be forgiven for viewing this information with some certain suspicion, for chieftains of the Yathoon have never been known to entertain friendly relations with the human beings who share their planet with them. And yet—and yet . . .

"Come to think of it," she whispered doubtfully, "I *have* heard it related that the two courtiers closest to the heart of Jandar of Shondakor are a swordmaster, whose natal city is my own—"

"My friend Lukor," nodded Koja. "With perhaps the single exception of Jandar himself, the finest swordsman on all of Thanator—"

"—and a renegade Yathoon," the girl finished breathlessly, "whose name I do not recall."

"Myself," said Koja solemnly.

"We must talk further of these matters," the Princess of Ganatol concluded doubtfully. Koja somberly agreed; he guessed that it had occurred to the Princess that he could have been an agent of Fanga, planted among the slaves to sniff out mischief by gaining the confidence of his fellow captives.

But there was nothing that he could think of to say that might reassure her.

While Koja found his new condition of slavery naturally irksome and degrading, Taran adjusted to the situation more easily and swiftly. Nobody paid any particular attention to the youngster. The reason for this was that to the Yathoon, an immature youth is not a full member of the tribal community, and is generally ignored and left to fend for himself.

Once beyond the years of infancy, the Yathoon young manage to attach themselves to the following of one of the warriors or chieftains, for whom they perform menial labor in exchange for training in the use of weapons. These adolescent Yathoon are considered "cadets," and barely possess a personal identity of their own in the eyes of their masters, who in the majority of cases do not even know their names: they are anonymous and virtually invisible. Taran fell into this classification.

He was mainly supposed to keep out of the way and not make a nuisance of himself. True, he was chained in the slave pens at night along with the other captives, but during the days he was seldom assigned to any work groups.

This left Taran comparatively free and unobserved, and gave him considerable freedom of movement. He soon attached himself to the Princess of Ganatol, to stay with her and assist her on those occasions when Koja was assigned elsewhere. Xara used these opportunities to question the boy, who spoke freely of Shondakor and carelessly confirmed Koja's high position at court and his close relationship with Jandar.

The boy was so open and guileless in his manner that even Xara could not believe him a dupe or a spy.

He was obviously what he said he was, which meant that Koja was, too. Xara began to feel ashamed of having entertained suspicions of the Yathoon warrior who had taken the blows of Hoog's whip in order to spare her that indignity.

Very soon, Koja and Taran and Xara formed a small nucleus of conspiracy within the body of the Garukh slaves. Borak found himself aligned with them, for, although such emotions as loyalty and friendship were alien and all but incomprehensible to such as he, self-interest provides a powerful incentive for learning new things. Certain common bonds of comradeship existed between Borak and Koja already, and these were further strengthened by their mutual determination to escape from slavery to Fanga.

It was these feelings that set them apart from the other slaves, and the very isolation they felt from the others drew them more closely together. The others who shared the slave pens with them were mostly Yathoon, with a sprinkling of human captives, Tharkolian, or Perushtarian, including a few of the Ku Thad who lived and hunted in the Grand Kumala. For the most part these others were a listless and dispirited lot who had been brutalized and depersonalized through years of hopeless captivity and unremitting toil until they were little more than beasts of burden, devoid of will or the power to make decisions on their own.

Escape was always a possibility, however remote, for two reasons. In the first place, the Garukh Clan was small in number and could spare few warriors for guard duty over the slave pens, and even fewer for sentry duty over the perimeter of the camp. Then again there was the inflexible Yathoon attitude toward slavery in general: a slave was a subhuman, a soulless thing, and the Yathoon considered them almost incapable of independent thought. Those of the slaves who were themselves Yathoon felt very much the same about their condition, which seemed to them hopeless.

The arthropods of Thanator share a deadly sense of fatalism, of Kismet, which saps the will and robs them of the ability to think and plan for themselves. From his years of associating with humans, Koja had largely outgrown this simplistic philosophy, but Borak felt it deeply. The former Haroob chieftain, however, had a powerful motive for freedom in his unsleeping desire to be revenged upon Gorpak and Hooka for their villainous treachery.

It was this hunger for vengeance that enabled Borak to shrug off the lethargic effects of *va lu rokka*. This phrase sums up the fatalistic philosophy which dominates the Yathoon race. It may be translated as "It was destined," and it is the stolid and uncomplaining Yathoon comment on each and every turn of events.

But Koja, Taran, and Xara did not believe *va lu rokka,* and persuaded Borak to join with them in seeking to escape. It did not prove very difficult, for Borak, like Koja, was more intelligent than most of his kind, more of an individual, capable of independent thought.

All that was needed was for the proper opportunity to present itself. Before this came about, however, Fate took another turn, and one that would probably prove to be for the worst.

For Fanga gave the command to break camp, and the Clan made ready to depart for the unknown south, where lay the secret heartland of the Yathoon race.

10

The Garukh Ride South

For two weeks we had flown south from Shondakor, searching the broad and fertile grasslands of the Great Plains of Haratha for some sign of our missing friends. Thus far, at least, our quest had proved futile, for no slightest sign had we yet discovered that would prove a clue to the whereabouts of Koja or Taran or the two *othodes*.

My personal squadron had now reached the middle point of the plains, halfway between Shondakor and the South Pole. From here the mighty prairie of crimson grasses stretched in every direction for hundreds of *korads*.

"The area is simply too vast for the squadron to search in formation," argued burly, truculent Ergon. "It is a waste of time and manpower, my lad—my Prince, I mean."

"If it is your considered opinion that we should split the squadron up and search in individual craft, friend Ergon," said Lukor of Ganatol spiritedly, "then I must agree with you, for your opinion concurs with mine own."

We had landed that eve on the shore of one of the twin rivers, had hunted down a herd of migrating *vanth* and made our kill, and were roasting dripping haunches of meat over a roaring bonfire while resting after the day's vigilance and toil.

My squadron is an honor guard composed of thirteen scoutcraft and my personal yacht, the *Shondakor*.

Generally, these ornithopters are manned by a select crew of Sky Navy personnel, assigned to the palace squadron according to a system of rotation. On this particular occasion, however, many of my friends and courtiers had volunteered to take part in the search. Among these were the bald, burly Perushtarian gladiator Ergon, with whom I had fought side by side in the Arena of Zanadar, and who had become one of my closest comrades. Lukor, of course, could not be left behind: the peppery, gallant little sword-master loved nothing more than a good fight, unless it was an adventure in which, at some point, a good fight might be expected to occur.

Prince Valkar, the stalwart young Shondakorian noble who was related to my Princess, also had joined the quest. We had met years before while both of us happened to be serving in the Chac Yuul, disguised as common mercenaries. As well, that scrawny guttersnipe Glypto was with us on this search, for as Kaamurath's master spy, the sharp-tongued and wily little thief had accompanied his royal master on his recent state visit to the Golden City of the Ku Thad.

Over our dinner we considered the problem of searching so vast an area as the entire southern hemisphere of Thanator with only fourteen ships, and argued the various points of view which were presented as, one by one, the glowing, multicolored moons ascended the skies like jack-o'-lanterns.

And by the time we were done and were ready to seek our cloaks for a well-earned night's sleep, we had reached the only reasonable solution to the problem that confronted us. We had resolved, in fine, to divide our squadron up, each craft to search by air a particular quadrant of the plains, with a point of rendezvous previously decided upon, where all ships would return to reunite the squadron.

If any ship did not return at the appointed time, that would constitute a signal that the craft had sighted something that might be a clue to the whereabouts of the missing friends we sought. A careful record was made of the territory assigned to each craft in the squadron so that we should at once know to which region we should direct our attentions should one of the craft fail to appear at the rendezvous at the appointed time.

Tomar and Glypto were to search in the north, while Lukor and Ergon would take the east. Valkar and I were assigned to search in the southern parts, while my other friends were given their duty in the west. Each of us rode alone in a separate craft, together with one Shondakorian officer, except of course for the *Shondakor,* for my sky-yacht required a full complement of a dozen crew, due to its size.

Shortly after dawn we arose, broke our fast, filled our waterskins at the shore of the river, entered our craft, and departed to take up the search again.

Valkar's companion, as it turned out, was a young officer named Kadar. Together they flew directly into the southwest, since the *Shondakor* was to cover the southeastern region of the plains. There was little conversation between them, for both were too busy searching the limitless plain of scarlet meadowland beneath their hurtling craft to waste words. They flew at the modest height of one hundred and fifty feet, for at so low an altitude the smallest object would be clearly visible, and by flying at this height they hoped to be able to spy the most minute scrap of wreckage from the *Lankar-jan.*

They found instead a woeful and hungry and miserably lonely survivor of the lost expedition.

It was Fido the *othode!*

* * *

Landing, they tethered their craft to some bushes which grew atop a low rise of hills, and Valkar swung down to the ground on the rope ladder to be greeted by a hysterical *othode* pup.

Fido cavorted around the smiling Prince in a veritable ecstasy of happiness. The pup had deemed himself hopelessly lost and had been merely wandering in circles, mournfully hoping to find his lost people again. Now he went mad with joy, recognizing Valkar either on sight or because his smell was familiar. The Prince knelt to pet the wriggling *othode*, who crept to him on his belly, whimpering and complaining, then sprang into the Prince's arms, wetting his face with slobbering kisses.

"There, there, Fido," chuckled Valkar, struggling to calm the wriggling armful of hysterically happy *othode*. "It's all right—good boy, Fido—good pup—calm down, now, and tell me all about it!"

Once the pup had calmed down a bit and had hungrily devoured a portion of the remnants of yesterday evening's *vanth* steak, Prince Valkar and Kadar tried to coax Fido to lead them to Taran and Koja. The pup was agreeable but bewildered, not able to comprehend what his human friends desired of him. He charged off gleefully in this direction or that at Valkar's urging, only to stop after a bit and turn, to squat with lolling tongue and eager eyes, awaiting instructions on the rest of the game.

Eventually, Valkar and Kadar had to give up.

"A pity the boy or Bozo never taught Fido how to track," sighed the young officer. "*Othodes* are considered to have a most sensitive and keen sense of smell, and can track game for many *korads*. Fido, however, doesn't even seem to understand what it is we desire of him."

"I'm afraid you're right," admitted the Prince

wryly. "At least, we have found Fido, which suggests that Koja and Taran probably came this far, which means they may be somewhere in this vicinity."

"Yes, my Prince," nodded the lieutenant. "But, on the other hand, suppose Fido and Bozo merely went off by themselves, and that their leaving the city had absolutely nothing to do with Taran and Koja's flight. In that case, finding Fido may have no connection at all with our hopes of finding the boy and his Yathoon friend!"

"You could be right, of course," said Valkar. "Still and all, having found Fido is better than finding nothing at all."

"If I may make a suggestion then, my Prince," murmured the young officer diffidently, "let us take to the air again and search the area in ever-widening circles, using a spiral search pattern with the place where we spotted Fido as the center of the pattern."

"Not a bad idea," Valkar assented. "It's obviously hopeless to try to follow Fido's tracks in this thick grass, and he may have just been running in circles himself. Come, help me get him into the rear seat."

Fido proved rather recalcitrant and uncooperative, for the pup had unhappy memories of having recently ridden in one of these ornithopters and was reluctant to undergo such an experience again, if he had any say in the matter. Between the two of them, however, Prince Valkar and the young officer managed to man-handle the yelping and ungainly *othode* pup into the rear part of the cockpit, tethering him securely with the safety straps so that he could not jump out again.

Then they ascended to their former height and began to scrutinize the plain, searching in ever-expanding circles from the point where they had found the son of Bozo.

* * *

As for Bozo himself, the mighty *othode* had traversed the endless plains for sixteen days without discovering the slightest sign of his vanished friends.

In early morning, just before daybreak, he had come upon a nest of plump, timid *uggars* amidst the tall, dew-wet grasses. He had made his kill and had devoured the warm, fresh meat as if he were famished, which indeed he was. Then he had continued on at an easier, more comfortable pace until he succeeded in locating water. Once he had drunk his fill, the exhausted *othode* had rested for a time in the shade of thick-leaved low bushes which grew close to the ground.

Shortly after dawn, Bozo was suddenly aroused to full wakefulness from his weary slumber. The wary beast did not at once realize what it was that had triggered his awakening.

And then he felt it again, that faint, mysterious vibration in the ground itself.

Bozo lifted his head and cautiously sniffed the wind, but it was blowing from his back and even his sensitive nostrils could discern nothing.

Lying flat, the *othode* laid his ear against the ground and listened intently. A dull drumming, as of many feet pounding the earth. Dim thoughts moved through his puzzled brain. Was it perhaps the sound made by the hooves of a vast herd of *vanth,* for this was the season of the year during which the migrant herds of that elk-like animal are accustomed to wander the Great Plains in their numberless thousands.

Or was the distant vibration perhaps caused by a stampede of beasts, fleeing from advancing walls of flame? At times the endless leagues of scarlet grass catch fire, and the ensuing conflagration can rage on unchecked for days, scorching many square *korads* black with ash, driving all manner of plains-dwelling creatures before its inexorable advance. But Bozo could not discern the bitter and unmistakable aroma of burning grass upon the morning breeze.

Whatever it was, the sound was coming in his direction.

And—it was coming nearer all the time!

Half an hour, or a trifle later, Bozo's keen eyes saw a line of moving shapes upon the horizon. At length these moving objects became clearer, resolving into a rank of massive *glymphs*. These huge, ponderous, and lethargic beasts of burden, Bozo knew, are most commonly domesticated by man, and are used to draw wains, much in the manner of oxen.

Not that they resemble terrestrial oxen in the slightest, of course, for evolution has diverged widely on our two worlds. The *glymph* looks much more like the African rhinoceros, in fact, with a few details borrowed from an extinct species of dinosaur called triceratops. They are immense, heavy, lumbering, slow-footed creatures with a capacious bony shield which grows back from the skull to protect the back of their necks. The brow shield and their hooked, beak-like snouts are armed with sharp horns like the rhinoceros. Generally, their leathery hides are colored a dull slate-gray, which turns to pale yellowish white at throat and belly. This hide is spotted or sometimes striped and splotched with patches of an amazing bright red, as if some teenaged hoodlum had amused himself by tossing the contents of a can of red paint over the hapless *glymphs*.

Bozo watched the line of plodding *glymphs* from his place of concealment under the bushes.

Soon he discerned that the ponderous brutes were harnessed to enormous metal chariots wherein rode a number of tall, gaunt, stalk-legged Yathoon warriors armed with twenty-foot spears. Behind the row of chariots came herds of smaller, more fleet-footed *thaptors* ridden by cadets and less-important warriors,

servitors and artisans. Behind these came yet a second
rank of *glymphs,* dragging huge, cumbersome wains
which were filled with gear, folded tents, and stacked
weapons.

And slaves . . .

A whimper of eagerness broke from the throat of
Bozo the *othode.* But his instinct for caution over-
ruled his eagerness, and he lay without moving, concealed from the eyes of the Yathoon scouts and outriders by the shadows of the bushes and the thick
scarlet grasses.

The Yathoon caravan rolled slowly by and wound
its leisurely way to the south.

Only when it had receded far to the south did Bozo
emerge from his place of concealment. He stood for
a long moment, staring after the caravan as it dwin-
dled from sight under the golden skies of Thanator.

Then he turned south and began to follow it at a
tireless lope.

For among those slaves bundled together in the
mighty wains, his keen eyes had recognized the features of Taran and Koja.

BOOK THREE

INTO THE
UNKNOWN SOUTHLANDS

11

Slaves of the Horde

Fanga's command to strike the camp and depart for the south came as no surprise. Everyone had been expecting it to be ordered by the chief at any time.

Even Taran, who had little experience in the ways of the savage Yathoon Horde, knew that the regions around the southern pole were completely under the domination of the emotionless arthropods. There they ruled supreme, and in those parts of Callisto there were no human cities to challenge their supremacy.

He knew also that somewhere in the unknown southland the Yathoon Horde guarded jealously the secret place they considered to be their sacred homeland. The youngster thought it likely that this was the place called "Sargol," to which he had previously heard the Yathoon warriors and chieftains make cryptic reference.

As he was not certain but was curious about it, he queried Koja on this very point.

The arthropod did not change expression, but he was not too happy at Taran's question. Sargol, and the secret it contained, was precious to his race. It was not something Koja felt himself to be at liberty to

discuss openly with anyone who did not belong to
the Yathoon.

It was precisely here that Koja's loyalties were
divided. The Horde itself might consider him to be
a renegade, an outlaw, but from Koja's own point of
view, he was not truly *aharj*. Koja had not been out-
lawed by the Kandars, and neither had he been driven
into exile. He had freely chosen to depart, and had
followed Jandar on his adventures because he wished
to, not because no other alternative existed.

Jandar had taught Koja the meaning of friendship. That friendship seemed to Koja at the time, as
it seemed to him now, more precious and valuable
even than membership in the mighty Yathoon Horde.

Thus his feelings toward his own kind were, to say
the least, equivocal. He did not consider himself to
be at enmity with the other insect-men: he still
thought of himself as one of them, although he had
come to live apart from the great tribes of his kind.
Therefore, to Koja's way of thinking, the secrets of
the Yathoon race were still his secrets to keep.

On the other hand, Taran would soon enough perceive the wonders of Sargol, for the Garukhs were
headed there, so there did not seem to be any particular reason to refuse the boy the information that
he sought.

He decided to temporize, to say as little as was
possible, without seeming to be abrupt or secretive.

"Sargol is the name by which we call the place to
which we are going," he said solemnly.

"I thought so," Taran exclaimed triumphantly.
"But, Koja-*chan,* is Sargol the name of the whole
southland where the Yathoon roam and live, or just
one particular part of it?"

"It is one particular part of it," admitted Koja.

Xara of Ganatol, who lay chained near them, and
who had been listening to their conversation with
interest, now spoke up with a question of her own.

"Is it where your females are kept, Koja?" the. Princess inquired. "And the young of your race, as well? For I assume that you keep your females and their children in one particular place, since none are here with the Clan. They can only be living somewhere in the south . . ."

Koja solemnly agreed that this was the case. But he did not wish to go into further details, and Borak, who lay nearby and who was also listening, spoke up then and came to his rescue by diverting the conversation to another subject.

The Yathoon nation is divided into four great Clans, the Zajjadar, the Angkang, the Haroob, and the Kandar, and two smaller Clans, more recently formed, the Thoromé and the Garukh.

Each Clan has its own high chief, or *akka-komor*, but over them all is one supreme autocrat, the Arkon, or Emperor.

The Arkon and his court are resident in Sargol, where they protect the Yathoon females and their young, and rule all of the southern hemisphere in a desultory fashion. Periodically, the Clans return to the southland to rest, to refurbish their weapons, to lie with the females and thus beget their young. After these brief periods, they return to the outside world in their mighty caravans to hunt for food, which they preserve in a manner peculiar to their kind.

They return with these fruits of the hunt to Sargol, to replenish the supplies of nutriment upon which the Yathoon young and the females depend. For there exists no edible game in the frigid regions of the south, and were the great caravans not to return to Sargol, those who dwell in the sacred homeland would at length perish from starvation.

Once they are beyond that invisible barrier that Yathoon tradition has established as the limit of their southerly domain, each Clan and tribe considers itself at war with every other Clan or tribe, or at least in a posture of armed and wary enmity. But once within the southern regions again, an absolute and ironclad truce is considered to exist, and no male Yathoon is permitted to slay or to attack another male on any conceivable pretext, upon pain of death in the Arena.

This is called the Peace of Sargol, and it has never been broken.

It is obvious to any student of cultures that some such arrangement would have to exist, for otherwise one Clan could seize and occupy Sargol to the exclusion of all other Clans and tribes. They would then possess all of the Yathoon females, and they alone would be able to breed and to beget the next generation.

The Yathoon, you understand, do not mate for life. Instead, they hold their females in common and compete in games of warfare or athletic prowess for the attentions of the females, and for the privilege of lying with them and of begetting offspring.

Each champion, and several of the runners-up, have their choice of females during the period in which their Clan observes the Peace of Sargol. The larva laid by the females are then marked with the Clan or tribal totem mark of the champion who was the parent. When the young are hatched, they are trained for survival, and when they are old enough to begin training for war, they enter the retinues of the various chieftains of their parent tribe or Clan, and are thought of as cadets.

But none of these young ever know their father's name, nor even the name of their mother. Parenthood is considered a duty and a privilege, but it remains an anonymous one. The reasons for this are obscure and lost in the mists of dim, forgotten ages.

Since they are born to females they can never identify, of a parentage forever unknowable to them, the warriors of the Yathoon never experience the emotions of filial devotion or love. You cannot love a father whose name is unknown to you, nor a mother you have never seen. You can feel no brotherly love for your siblings if you have no way of ever knowing which of the other young in your nest are your own brothers and sisters.

Thus the love between mates, and the love a parent feels for its child, and the emotions which commonly bind children of one family together are completely unknown to the pitiful, cold, ever-emotionless barbarians who inhabit the frigid southlands, who roam and rule the measureless plains, and who live out their empty and loveless lives in an eternal war against every other thing that lives.

Camp was broken, as it had been broken ten thousand times before and would be broken ten thousand times again. The tents were dismantled and packed away in the covered wains. The *thaptor* pens were taken apart pole by pole, lashed into bundles, and strapped to the backs of the mighty *glymphs*. The caravan was at last ready to depart.

Every Yathoon warrior knew precisely what his duties and responsibilities were, and fulfilled them to the letter. The chieftains mounted their *thaptors* and rode in the fore, followed by the hunters and warriors and cadets of their households. The wains, which contained their baggage, their treasure, their weapons, and their slaves, followed the retinue.

The caravan wound slowly across the Great Plains of Haratha, winding ever south. As the territories traditionally under the dominence of this or that Clan or tribe of the Horde are widely set apart from each other, it did not seem very likely that the Garukhs would encounter one of their rival Yathoon Clans on their southerly migration, but should this occur it was almost inevitable that war would flare up between them. For this reason, and so as to afford his warriors

the greatest possible margin of advantage, the high
chief, Fanga, sent outriders before the caravan and to
all sides, ranging far afield to scout out any approaching enemy.

All that day they journeyed south, moving with all
deliberate speed but in no particular hurry. In fact,
the Clan could move no more swiftly than they did,
due to the ponderous and lumbering *glymphs* which
dragged the great wains behind them. The huge,
oxenlike beasts were slow-moving and heavy-footed,
and they could not be hurried. The Clan must perforce reduce its speed to the pace at which the
glymphs could comfortably advance.

That night they made temporary camp on the
Great Plains, choosing their location around a water-
hole which the Garukhs had noticed months before,
when first they had ridden out into these parts. Even
though the encampment was to be a temporary one
and their stay here was one of only nocturnal dura-
tion, the tents were erected and the *thaptor* pens were
set up again just as they had been at the last camp,
where they had remained for many weeks.

The Yathoon warriors knew no other way of doing
things than the way things were always done amongst
them. In this, as in so many other ways, the intelligent
arthropods resembled their distant cousins, the social
insects of my own native world. Like the ants and
bees and termites of Earth, which had evolved a rudimentary social organization aeons in the past, found
that it worked well enough, and simply maintained
it without ever making experiments or attempting to
improve the system, the Yathoon of the Horde did not
ever question immemorial tradition or tamper with
the customary way of doing things perfected unguess-
able ages ago by their remotest ancestors.

No more conservative creatures existed than the
Yathoon arthropods. And in that very inflexibility of
their thinking, in their innate inability to change, to

adapt, to grow into new social configurations with the arising of new circumstances, lay the seeds of their eventual doom. For no social order is so flawlessly perfect that it cannot be improved, or so ideally organized that it cannot break down. By now unable to change—unable even to imagine the necessity for change, and probably unable even to recognize change when it is forced upon them—the Yathoon were slowly dying, as their world changed around them.

The spread of manned air flight is one of the ways in which Thanator was changing, for instance. Valkar and the young lieutenant Kadar had searched all that day the region of the grasslands which stretched out to every side from the position in which they had found Fido earlier. They had flown in an ever-widening spiral, using that spot as a starting point, and just after nightfall the path of their circling flight intercepted the route of the southerly migration of the Garukh nomads.

The keen eyes of Kadar had first seen the track of the *glymphs,* for the heavy-footed and ponderous creatures had beaten a pathway through the wild grasses. But the Yathoon scouts had not seen the little aircraft as it floated far above them, although the sound of its engines was clearly audible to their sense of hearing.

They did not look up because they were not accustomed to looking up, there never having been in the experience of their ancestors much of anything to look up for.* Thus, although they clearly heard the

*Thanator has no flying creatures of any particular number, save for small aerial lizards like seagulls and one dangerous species of flying predator, the *ghastozaar,* which hunts singly and is unlikely to attack any large body of warriors. The depredations of the Sky Pirates of Zanadar were mostly limited to the northern hemisphere of Callisto and rarely troubled the Horde. The winged Zarkoon savages infest only the Far Side of the planet.

roaring of the scoutcraft's engines, they had no idea what caused the sound and dismissed it as being of no particular importance. The Yathoon are not a very imaginative race.

Cutting their engines, Prince Valkar and Kadar let their ornithopter drift idly with the breeze, while spying out the Yathoon encampment. It was too dark for them to make out any particular individuals—so dark that they could scarcely tell the arthropods from their human slaves. They were undecided as to what to do.

"Do you think it likely, my Prince, that Koja and the boy were taken captive by the Horde?" murmured Kadar as they floated above the camp.

"It seems very likely to me," confessed the Prince grimly. "Fido came from somewhere in this area, and if Koja and Taran crashed here, they could easily have been spotted by the Yathoon scouts." His expression became grimmer, as he added by way of an after-thought: "Of course, they weren't necessarily captured at all. They could as easily have been slain . . ."

"What does my Prince suggest we do now?" asked Kadar.

"We wait," said Valkar. "We can discover little of importance by night, but with day we may be able to ascertain if, indeed, our friends are prisoners of the Horde."

The wind had died and the air above the Great Plains was all but motionless. Prince Valkar did not dare try to bring the scoutcraft down so as to anchor it to the surface of the meadow, lest Yathoon sentinels should perceive their actions and attack them. So he and Kadar made a makeshift meal of cold meats, refreshed themselves with water from the canteens, shared their stores of provender with the miserable Fido, who was now heartily weary of being airborne, and curled up in the cockpit for the night, wrapping their cloaks about them for warmth.

* * *

When day broke in the skies above Thanator in that vast, silent explosion of light that is dawn on the Jungle Moon, the two questors awoke to discover that they had floated a mile or two south of the encampment of the Horde, but found it easy enough to find the camp again.

The Garukhs were in the process of breaking camp, loading their gear back in the wains, and entering formation again. Valkar took the little scoutcraft up to far greater altitude than that at which they had flown previously, while searching for some sign of their lost comrades. He did this in order to mitigate their chances of being seen, and also because it was no longer necessary to search for Koja and Taran.

Because they had found them. In the clear golden light of morning both captives had been sighted as they labored in the chains of the Horde.

The caravan rode south, and above them all the way soared the scoutcraft, while aboard two worried Shondakorians strove to figure out a way to rescue Koja and Taran from their captivity.

12

Thundering Hooves

All that day the little scoutcraft followed in the wake of the Yathoon caravan, while the migratory Clan stolidly pursued its southward way.

Since the Shondakorian ornithopter had fortunately thus far eluded discovery by the Yathoon scouts and outriders, Prince Valkar and the young officer took every precaution to make certain that their very existence remained a secret. The advantage of surprise, they reasoned, might yet prove vital to the success of their plans.

But the trouble was, they really had no plans. Once they had found out that Koja and young Taran still lived and were presently the captives of the Yathoon caravan, they bent every thought to the conception of a method by which the two might be rescued from their insectoid captors. As yet, however, no viable scheme for the rescue had occurred to either of them.

They could not simply engage the migratory Clan in battle, of course. Few activities are more intrinsically suicidal than for two warriors and a half-grown *othode* pup to challenge the might of a force of enemy swordsmen armed, so to speak, to the teeth, and numbering in the hundreds. Even the advantage they possessed in being able to attack from the air would afford them little more than a momentary tactical superiority which would soon be lost in the struggle against overwhelming numerical strength.

Neither could they swoop down and carry off the two prisoners by any conceivable means, since both Koja and young Taran were chained to their fellow captives.

"If we could stage a diversion of some sort," suggested Kadar tensely, "while the attention of the guards was diverted, one or the other of us could descend by means of the mooring cable and perhaps sever the chains, or pry them apart, and then Koja and the boy could climb up the cable and we could all fly away together . . . ?"

"What sort of a diversion?" asked Valkar practically.

"Um," replied the lieutenant lamely, subsiding into thoughtful silence.

"Perhaps," remarked Kadar a bit later, "once darkness falls, we could set the meadow grasses afire, and while the Yathoon are busy fighting the fire, we could come down and carry off our friends unseen in the gloom of night?"

"Perhaps," nodded the Prince with a marked lack of enthusiasm. "But suppose the wind changes and the fire turns back and goes the other way? Or suppose the Yathoon simply decided to out-race the flames? Or suppose it is the captives they send out in front of the warriors to fight the fire?"

"Um," said the lieutenant for a second time. Again he lapsed into moody silence, a silence which upon this occasion continued unbroken for a goodly time.

"There must be some way we can use the ornithopter to good advantage," Valkar mused. "It seems foolish to have this unique aerial superiority, without somehow putting it to use. But, for the life of me, I have to confess I cannot envision any method of rescuing our friends from the air which is not obviously foredoomed to failure . . ."

The young officer nodded gloomily, saying nothing. The trouble was that the flying machine was exceptionally vulnerable to damage when used at close grips with an enemy such as the Yathoon barbarians. A single lucky arrow-strike or spear-cast, and the pontoons of levitating gas upon which the aerial contrivance rode would be punctured, causing a serious loss of irretrievable gas. The twenty-foot spears wherewith the arthropods were armed were deadly weapons in their hands, and could be thrown for enormous distances and with uncanny accuracy. The same danger was attached to their mighty war bows and the barbed arrows which each warrior carried and with whose use the Yathoon were experienced from the egg, so to speak.

They flew on all that day, following the rear guard of the migrating clan, and when darkness fell they still had not conceived of a plan for the rescue of their friends that had the slightest chance of succeeding.

Ironically enough, at the same time that Prince Valkar and his lieutenant were racking their brains to think of some plan for rescuing their friends from their plight, Koja and his fellow captives were similarly engaged.

Chained together in the wains with the other slaves, they conversed by whispers pitched too low to attract the attention of the other captives. It had occurred to Koja that unique and favorable opportunities for making their escape were open to them, now that the Horde was on its great southward trek. That is to say, during the migration virtually the entire attention of their guards was focused on the dangers that might threaten from without. Busied with watching for the approach of enemies from elsewhere upon the Great

Plains, they were less alert and wary in guarding their captives.

In part this was due to the difficulty of trying to do two different things at the same time. But another element was the peculiarly Yathoon attitude toward slaves, which I have already described. A slave is an item of property, soulless and devoid of rights; and, moreover, a slave possesses no freedom of will, being completely subject to the whims or wishes of his master. To the coldly logical brains of the Yathoon, it is hard to conceive of a slave seeking his freedom. How can a piece of property be capable of such independence of thought? To the Yathoon way of thinking, an escaped slave is almost a contradiction in terms. And such is the grimly fatalistic philosophy to which they adhere that most of the Yathoon slaves, being themselves of the Yathoon race, unconsciously share the same outlook.

But young Taran and Xara of Ganatol were of a different breed from the Yathoon, and were in no way subject to this bleak and hopeless philosophy. And Koja, although a Yathoon born and bred, had been exposed for so long a time to different modes of thought that his adherence to the beliefs of his kind had deeply eroded. And as for Borak, such was the strength of his desire for revenge upon his enemies that he had been persuaded to abandon *va lu rokka* for freedom of will.

And if ever they were to make their escape, it was now. Now or never, in fact: for with every league that they continued to be carried southward in their chains, they came closer to Sargol.

And escape from the Hidden Valley, whose every point of egress was heavily guarded by alert warriors, Koja knew, simply was beyond the realm of the possible.

What was needed, Koja and his fellow conspirators at length decided, was a diversion.

This was precisely the same decision that Valkar
and Kadar simultaneously had reached.

But—*what* diversion, and how arranged, and by
whom to be set into action?

It was the day following the discussion by Koja
and the others of this aspect of their escape that Fate,
or Destiny, intervened.

The first sign that Koja or his comrades had that
Fate had decided to intervene on their behalf came
in the form of a distant sound of drumming.

At first it was but faintly audible over the sounds
of the wains creaking, the wind in the long crimson
grass, and the heavy, lumbering tramping of the feet
of the *glymphs*. But gradually it became louder as
it came nearer, until at length it was noticed by all.
It sounded like ten thousand tomtoms beaten all at
once with an irregular rhythm.

Scouts and outriders craned to look in every direction, searching the horizon for the source of this
mysterious and omnipresent sound. Like the steady
roar of the surf it was, but here there were no seas.
Like the drumming of a thousand hoofs it was, but
if that was the explanation of the sound, which grew
louder and louder with every passing moment, then
where were the beasts whose pounding hooves were
the cause of that drumming?

Then, like a long wall of smoke athwart the horizon, stretching from north to south, a cloud of dust
became visible. And the outriders of the Horde, who
had observed such phenomena before, knew the origin
of that distant drumming and realized at last their
danger.

For it was a vast and numberless herd of *vanth*
hurtling across the plains in the direction of the
Garukh caravan. As yet there was no clue as to the
nature of the disturbance, but a stampede is a stampede, and no matter what it was that had disturbed

the herds of the *vanth* and had panicked them into flight, in flight they surely were, in all their thousands.

The Great Plains of Haratha experience no phenomena more perilous or more deadly than a stampede of the *vanth*. So vast are the herds of these huge, staglike quadrupeds that, once goaded into mass flight, there is no barrier that can stand before them untrampled, save for the very mountains of the south themselves. Whole encampments of the Horde have vanished from knowledge because they stood in the way of such a stampede. No army, however barricaded, could have stood in their path for long.

And now the caravan in which Koja and Borak and Taran and Xara were captives stood directly in the path of the mightiest stampede of the *vanth* that could be imagined. Ten or twelve thousand of the mammoth heavy-footed beasts, maddened into flight by some still unknown cause, came thundering down upon the caravan like a living ocean of hurtling flesh from which no escape was possible or even imaginable.

As for the caravan, it simply disintegrated, the warriors riding off in any direction—as long as it was not in the direction from which the herds came thundering—without a moment's thought or hesitation.

The *glymphs* trumpeted in elephantine alarm and galloped off on their own, dragging their heavy wains behind them.

The thundering hooves were very near now, and the air darkened as immense clouds of dust veiled the sky.

The wain in which Koja and the others were chained was being dragged behind a team of panicky runaway *glymphs*. The Yathoon driver had leaped from the front of the wain and vanished in the whirling dust.

Bumping along over the swishing grasses, the wain

began to strike against rocks, for the land was rising
here into low, rocky hills. One such collision smashed
a wheel to flying fragments; then the axle shattered
against another boulder, and the wain began to break
apart. The wooden guard-rail which ran around the
sides of the wain, to which the captives were help-
lessly roped, also came apart, shattering into several
pieces from the impact of collision with the boulder.

Koja knew nothing. Then, a moment later, he
found himself lying on the grass, his tether fastened
to a stump of wood. He was groggy but unharmed,
and realized that he had been thrown clear when
the wain had broken apart.

But where were his friends?

He came to his feet, peering around through the
dust, but saw no one. Here and there he spotted a
fragment of the wain, but naught else. And the fore-
most of the stampeding *vanths* were almost upon him.
Another moment and he would be a mangled thing,
beaten into pulp beneath a thousand thudding
hooves.

But there, just ahead, was the huge boulder into
which the unruly *glymphs* had dragged the wain in
their mad flight. It was nearly as tall as a man, and
might afford him a momentary respite. He sprang
agilely upon its crest. And then the herd was upon
him, like a savage sea, waves of squealing, wild-eyed
vanth curling about the sides of the great rock. Deafened by the tumult, blinded by the whirling dust
which suddenly turned day into night, he reeled and
fell—

—And found himself astride the back of a great
bull *vanth*, legs locked instinctively about the beast's
barrel, clinging for life itself to the branching antlers
of its staglike crest!

Scarcely noticing its rider, the *vanth* hurtled forward.

Then, out of the seething murk of darkness, a tall,

gaunt figure staggered into view, directly in the path
of the charging *vanth* to whose back Koja clung.

Swifter than thought itself he recognized the figure
as that of Borak. It lurched, stumbling, into the path
of the *vanth* and raised its arms. Momentarily diverted, the *vanth* veered to one side, narrowly missing
the Yathoon. Without conscious volition, Koja bent—
caught Borak by the arm—drew him up astride the
charging bull.

They clung together, dust-covered, deafened, and
blinded, unable to think or to speak.

Moments later their exhausted beast foundered among
the rocky hills. As they tumbled clear, it fell on one
side, vanishing beneath the driving hooves of the
beasts close-packed behind it.

The two warriors clambered to the peak of the hill
and lay there, panting. All about them and to every
side a dust-gray sea of exhausted beasts raced by.
Many staggered and fell, to be trampled to a pulp in
moments. Others showed red, glazed eyeballs, tongues
lolling, mouths flecked with foam; soon they, too,
would fall to be trodden down by those behind them.

And then, almost as swiftly as it had broken upon
them, the storm passed. Suddenly, with magical swiftness, the herd melted away and was gone, dwindling
across the plain. Koja and Borak stood, peering
through the dusty murk; the plain was naught but
bare, trampled earth as far as either of them could
see. They could no longer discern the wreckage of
the wain, nor any sign of man. Here and there, like
driftwood cast up by a freak swirling of the tide, the
carcass of a dead beast lay in its gory ruin.

The thundering of thousands of hooves faded into
the distance.

Gradually, the thick mantle of dust, swept away by
the wind, cleared from the golden sky.

The stampede had come and gone, and they were miraculously unhurt.

But—*what of their comrades?*

Borak, doubtless, felt little concern for their where-abouts or safety, viewing their demise with the cold indifference of his stolid kind. But a poignant pang of sorrow and of sharp loss pierced the less armored breast of Koja at the thought of young Taran or fair Xara trampled to death under the flying hooves of the *vanth*.

But dead they were, must be, along with all of the Clan that had captured them . . .

Suddenly there appeared, riding across the beaten earth of the denuded plain, a line of tall huntsmen of the Yathoon, mounted on *thaptors*.

Koja and Borak would have concealed themselves to elude discovery, but already it was too late. Nocked arrows were pointed in their direction, and riders were already detaching themselves from the line to gallop forward and take them prisoner.

Out of the frying pan and into the fire is a phrase uniquely terrestrial in its connotations, but the sense of it would have been readily obvious to Koja, under the present circumstances. With the stoic indifference of his kind, he stood tall with his head high, arms folded upon his mighty breast, awaiting capture. Flight was a folly and escape an impossibility, and to have fought with bare hands would have been suicidal.

The Yathoon huntsmen came riding up to the foot of the hill whereon the two comrades stood. Dismounting, the hunters ascended the slope to secure their captives.

And Koja was never so surprised in all of his life as when the huntsmen knelt before him to lay their swords at his feet.

13

Duel to the Death

The huntsmen whom Koja and Borak so dramatically
encountered were a party of the Kandar Clan. This
Koja knew instantly, for he recognized their tribal
markings. What he did not at once grasp was the
reason for the welcome afforded him, which was, to
say the least, unexpectedly hospitable.

The leader of the hunting party he also recognized,
one Izon, who had been a cadet in Koja's own retinue,
but who now, it seemed, belonged to the retinue of
a rival chieftain named Gamchan.

Izon assisted Koja and Borak to fresh mounts, apparently taking it for granted that Koja wished to be
escorted back to the encampment of the Horde. Koja
wisely kept his silence; it would seem obvious that
many changes had taken place in the Clan leadership
since he had last been seated in its councils.

As for Borak, he took his cue from Koja and turned
an impassive face to all of these things, saying nothing.

"It has been long since last we met, Izon," observed
Koja as they rode from the trampled field. "How did
you come to belong to the retinue of Gamchan?"

"When you were captured by the flying ships, my
komor, the chieftain Gamchan laid instant claim to

your trove. Since none cared to challenge him, all that my *komor* had possessed, as well as all of those who had once followed him into battle, soon came under the chieftaincy of Gamchan."

"I see," mused Koja grimly. He well remembered the villainous Gamchan, his most jealous and treacherous rival in the Clan. The other had been second only to Koja in wealth, authority, and prestige, and had long desired to be first. Evidently, the dreams of Gamchan had come true.

"Does Pandol still lead the Clan?" he inquired.

"He leads no longer," said Izon heavily. "He was challenged by Gamchan to the *duello* two years ago, and fell before his steel. Some there are that claim the chieftain waited until the *akka-komor* was far gone in drink before daring to challenge him. At any rate, Gamchan is now *akka-komor* of the Kandars."

"Do you think he will be pleased or displeased when he learns that I have returned?" inquired Koja wryly.

The huntsman shrugged with a forward twitching of his knobbed antennae.

"He will be displeased, of course, for Gamchan has always feared and hated you, my *komor*," he replied tonelessly.

"Why, then, did you offer me the salute due to a chieftain of the Horde, rather than taking me prisoner, which you could easily have done, since I bear no arms?" asked Koja.

"You were my *komor* once," said Izon expressionlessly, "and you are still a *komor* of the Clan: how then could I deal toward you with disrespect?"

Koja said nothing, and they rode in silence for a time while he digested this valuable information.

The most surprising thing about it all was that Gamchan had not named him an outlaw. Nor, for that matter, had Pandol. This was truly a revelation to Koja, who had long since assumed that the warriors of his Clan had known or guessed that he had assisted Jandar and the Princess Darloona to escape. Now matters were cast in a completely different light, and suddenly the pattern became clear.

Something more than three and a half years before, Koja had permitted Jandar to escape from the captivity of the Horde; encountering Darloona in the jungles of the Grand Kumala, Jandar and the Princess did not enjoy freedom for very long, soon being recaptured by the Yathoon warriors. This time they were the slaves of Gamchan, a rival chieftain who had envied Koja his ownership of so rare an *amatar* as a human with yellow hair and blue eyes.

Gamchan had been struck down by Jandar in a quarrel; later, he had been about to deal "justice" to the rebellious slave who had dared to lift his hand against his master, but a sudden raid by the ornithopters of Prince Thuton, lord of the Sky Pirates, had thrown the encampment into turmoil; in the ensuing confusion, Koja had assisted the two humans to escape. All three had been captured by the Sky Pirates and were carried off together to Zanadar, the City in the Clouds.*

Now Koja realized that, in the confusion of the aerial attack, none of his fellow clansmen had noticed aught more than that Koja and the two humans had been captured by the Sky Pirates. Koja's true role in their escape had gone unguessed. Therefore, he had never been declared *aharj* and still retained his rank among the Kandars, although it was doubtless believed that he was long since dead.

A chieftain retains his rank in the Horde until death, or until he has either been defeated by a challenger or has been officially declared an outlaw for some crime.

* These events are given in fuller detail in the book *Jandar of Callisto*, the first volume in this series.

This simple fact totally altered the present circumstances. Suddenly, and most unexpectedly, Koja had found allies. And all might yet be well . . .

They entered the earthworks which surrounded the vast encampment of the Kandar Clan and at once made their way to the center of the camp, where Gamchan the high chief reposed.

There were many who recognized Koja as he rode through the rows of tents toward the residence of the *akka-komor*. And doubtless, in their coldly logical and unemotional way, there were many who were pleased at Koja's return.

In his day he had been the mightiest chieftain of the Clan, second only to Pandol the high chief himself. As a chieftain of twenty tents, Koja had commanded a princely retinue, and his *amatara*—his treasure trove—was second to none.

Among the greatest chieftains of his Clan, he had been a warrior of high renown and a huntsman of enviable skill.

It was only natural, then, for the Kandars to be pleased at his miraculous return from the dead.

Gamchan, however, was not pleased at all. When he emerged from his tent at the exact center of the encampment and received the salute of Koja, he was about as surprised as a Yathoon can be. But he tried not to show it, as all of the chieftains and captains of the Kandars were in audience upon the scene.

"How is it that the former chieftain Koja returns to us after so long a time?" demanded Gamchan. "We believed you either enslaved by the Zanadarians or slain by them years ago."

"I was indeed carried off into the captivity of the Sky Pirates," replied Koja calmly, "and was long a slave in their city, toiling as a gladiator in the great Arena of Zanadar."

"How, then, come you here?"

Koja shrugged. "In time there was a slave revolt, and in the battle I managed to escape," he said simply. Gamchan looked dubious, as if guessing that Koja had left very much unsaid.

"And since then?" he prompted.

"My wanderings have been many," said Koja expressionlessly, "and my adventures beyond the telling. Until just recently, I dwelt in Shondakor among the Ku Thad. Then, by an unhappy turn of Fate, I fell into the clutches of the Garukhs, who hold all of the Kandars in deadly enmity, as you know."

"I know it well," said Gamchan harshly. "It was that black devil Fanga who most opposed me for the high chieftaincy of the Kandars, even in view of my victory over Pandol in the *duello!* Tell me more. How did you escape from the villainous Garukhs, O Koja?"

Koja explained, having elicited the information from Izon during their journey hither. A hunting party of the Kandars had been organizing a drive of the *vanth* herds when one of the campfires ignited an accidental conflagration in the long prairie grasses, causing the mammoth herds, already in motion, to panic into a stampede. That stampede had shattered the Garukh caravan, destroying them utterly.

Gamchan looked mightily pleased at this information.

"Then the jealous and vindictive Fanga was trampled into red slime beneath the heavy hooves of the *vanth* herds, driven by my own proud and loyal Kandars?" he repeated gloatingly. "And he and all his warriors are slain?"

"I have no certain knowledge of the fact," admitted Koja, "but I do not know how any of them could have escaped. I and my comrade here"—he indicated Borak with a gesture—"only narrowly escaped being trampled to death ourselves."

Gamchan exclaimed in satisfaction.

"Then you return to us, O Koja, the bearer of

excellent news! And we are pleased to welcome the former chieftain back to his people. Your 'comrade,' as you call him, will become one of my slaves. As for yourself, we can use you among the hunters, and with steady luck and faithful service you may again rise to a chieftaincy among us—"

"I am already a chieftain of the Kandars and will remain one until my death," Koja interrupted in a cold, level tone of voice. "You know as well as do I that this is the Law of the Clan, O Gamchan! I am a *komor* senior in rank to yourself, having attained to that rank long before you. Once it became mine, no one can deprive me of it."

A murmur of agreement ran around the circle of listeners. But Gamchan looked surly and threatening, and it subsided.

"How can you be a chieftain, with no retinue to follow you in battle?" he asked skeptically.

Then it was that Borak spoke up.

"As for myself, I would rather walk in the retinue of Koja than be a slave in the shadow of Gamchan," he said.

Others came forward, and among them were some of those who had served in the retinue of Koja aforetime as full-fledged warriors, like Sujat, or cadets like Izon.

"I, too," said Izon, "would be numbered again in the retinue of Koja, my *komor*."

"And I," said Sujat and the others.

Gamchan looked angry, and if it had been within the limitations of the Yathoon physiognomy to scowl, he would have scowled—and thunderously.

"Your *komor*, is it?" he rasped. "And who has ever heard of a *komor* without a *komor*'s trove?"

"I once had such a trove," said Koja steadily. "But it was taken by yourself, Gamchan, and I think unlawfully—"

"How so, 'unlawfully'?" demanded the high chief, glowering.

"According to the Law of the Clan," said Koja, "my trove is my own until I am bested in the *duello* by another, whereupon it becomes lawfully his. Or unless I die, whereupon another may lay claim to it, unless challenged. But I am not dead, Gamchan, and neither have you bested me in battle. Therefore, return to me my treasure—for, as you yourself have said, whoever heard of a chieftain without a chieftain's trove?"

At those words, stung to a fury and losing all control, the high chief roared out a choked challenge and sprang upon Koja, swinging high his whip-sword.

And Koja was, of course, unarmed.

Ducking under the blow, Koja lunged forward and unexpectedly seized Gamchan in his embrace, wrapping both long, segmented arms about the upper thorax of his foe. Gamchan was astonished at this, for it is not in the natural order of things for a Yathoon to do battle barehandedly, so to speak. He tried to give voice to this argument, but Koja cut him off in a novel and unexpected—and really quite efficient—manner. That is, with a right to the jaw that laid Gamchan on his back, stunned and blinking.

The sword had fallen from Gamchan's claw when he fell. Now Koja sprang upon his foe, and there ensued a free-for-all without parallel in the annals of Yathoon warfare.

And perhaps I should explain here that upon the Jungle Moon of Callisto the fine art of fisticuffs is completely unknown, for some reason. It was I, Jandar, who introduced to the Callistans the earthly sport of pugilism; I learned rough-and-tumble in a number of hard schools back on my native world, and retain the craft for use as a secret weapon, so to speak. On a planet of master swordsmen, not one among them

who knows how to use his fists, it often came in handy
to be able to use your fists in a pinch. I know of no
better ace to have up your sleeve when the chips are
down than to possess the skill to deal your opponent
a good right to the jaw.

And Koja had seen me in action in this fashion
many times. Obviously, he had picked up a few of my
tricks. And the clawlike hands of the Yathoon, armored in tough chitin until they resembled gloves
of chain mail, made them powerful weapons.

It did not take Koja very long to teach Gamchan
that it pays to know how to use your fists, especially
when jumped by someone who has a sword when you
do not.

Before long, it was over. Beaten into unconscious-
ness, Gamchan sprawled there at Koja's feet. And
then Koja broke his neck.

This may seem unsporting, but the Yathoon are
fighters born and bred, not sportsmen. They learned
in a hard school that the only safe enemy is a dead
one.

And Gamchan was now a *very* dead one.

The next morning the lords and chieftains of the
Kandars, in council assembled, debated the right of
Koja to assume the mantle of the high chieftaincy
which he had won from Gamchan in fair and honest
battle.

This was, for the most part, a mere formality. Seldom was the conqueror's right to inherit the rank of
the conquered seriously questioned. True, Fanga had
questioned it when Gamchan bested the former high
chief, Pandol, but then there had been certain irregularities suspected in the circumstances of that duel.

That is, Gamchan was thought to have waited until
Pandol was dead drunk before challenging him.

In the present case, the only irregularities which
had any bearing on the legitimacy of Koja's claim

were the doings of Gamchan, who had attacked an unarmed man without warning. As no one would reasonably have expected chivalry and honor from such as Gamchan—who was known as a braggart, a coward, and a bully—no one saw fit to contest Koja's claim.

That evening he was elevated to the rank of *akka-komor* before the assembled warriors of the clan, who hailed him.

Gamchan's passing displeased few, if any. He had not been very popular, and as *akka-komor* he had been a distinct failure. The Clan had suffered from his poor leadership, his hasty and rash decisions, and everyone felt safer and happier with Koja in his place.

Especially Koja.

That day and the next he investigated the warriors who had been in Gamchan's retinue, weeding out the ones known to be cowards or bullies or loafers, whom he replaced with those of his former followers who now flocked to join his new retinue. Among these were Izon and Sujat and Thomor and wise, canny old Zook.

And, of course, Borak.

Under the glory of the moons they conversed, Koja and Borak, while digesting the remnants of the victory feast.

"What do you intend doing now, O Koja?" inquired Borak. "Now you can return to Shondakor the Golden, for there are none with the authority to say you nay."

Koja was inwardly troubled. He yearned to see his friends again—that was only natural. But the trouble was, he was now responsible for the well-being of the Kandars. And Koja was one who took seriously his responsibilities.

"This was to be the last roundup of the *vanth*

before the Clan departed for the Secret Valley of Sargol," he observed in his flat, emotionless tones.

"That, I believe, is so," replied Borak. "But what
have you decided to do?"

Koja thought for a moment, then said:

"I will lead the Kandars into the Secret Valley now
that Taran and the Princess of Ganatol are dead."

And his tones were bleak and empty as he said
those words—almost as bleak and empty as his heart.

14

Wings of Rescue

However inescapable it may have seemed to Koja the Yathoon to suppose the boy Taran and the beautiful Princess of Ganatol had fallen beneath the thundering hooves of the maddened *vanth,* such, happily, was not the case.

From aloft in their small aerial scout, Prince Valkar and his lieutenant, Kadar, to say nothing of Fido the *othode,* had narrowly watched the progress of the caravan as it wound its meandering way across the limitless plain. And thus it was that from their lofty vantage they had been first to perceive the dreadful danger which impended; not even the scouts and outriders of the Horde, on their fleet, far-ranging *thaptors,* had espied the stampede before they.

Kadar, white to the lips, clutched Valkar by the upper arm and pointed off across the plain.

"Look!" he said huskily. Valkar followed his pointing finger and saw that long line of panic-maddened beasts—saw, too, that their inexorable advance was destined to swallow and to trample down the Yathoon caravan—and his heart sank within his breast.

But in the next instant he had kicked the scoutcraft into a hurtling dive. For, from his long association with me, Valkar of Shondakor had learned one of life's most important lessons: *never give up hope until the last instant of time, and strive to the very last, even against impossible odds.*

Thus it was that, when the thundering wall of stampeding *vanth* shattered in titanic collision with the Yathoon caravan, the small scoutcraft was winging low over the vehicles of the arthropods; and even as the wain in which our friends were riding broke up against the boulder, and Xara of Ganatol sprang free, clutching young Taran to her breast, she had no sooner touched the ground than the strong arms of Valkar swooped her up, and the lad, too, and bore them aloft to relative safety.

Valkar had flung down the rope ladder and clambered swiftly to the bottom rung, while Kadar clung to the controls. Now, as Valkar caught the two in his arms, Kadar kicked the rudder pedals and the game little craft arrowed upward again through the drifting clouds of dust raised by ten thousand pounding hooves. Below them, in whirling and half-glimpsed chaos, warriors and beasts screamed once and then were still, trampled into the dusty earth of the plain.

Xara gasped, cried out, and coughed dry dust from her lungs, staring incredulously as the prairie swung, then dipped and sank beneath her. She stared dazedly up into the tense, dust-covered features of the young prince, then aloft, and wonderingly, at the winged shape of his flying craft. Such as it she had seen many times in the past, for the Sky Pirates of Zanadar had long been a peril to her people. But her handsome and stalwart young rescuer was an absolute stranger to her, for never had she laid eyes upon him before.

It is, I think, a tribute to the womanly heart of Xara of Ganatol that even in such desperate straits as these—snatched from the very path of those horrendous hooves—she was not oblivious to the manly charm of her rescuer.

In the next instant the boy blinked wide-eyed, grinned enormously, and crowed at the top of his lungs—

"Valkar-*jan!*"

The prince hugged the boy briefly, then directed him to seize the rungs of the ladder while he assisted the girl to safety. The boy scooted up the rungs, nimble as a monkey, while Valkar and the princess ascended after him.

Valkar assisted the shaken Ganatolian girl to a seat in the craft and clambered in beside her. Taran, in the front seat beside the lieutenant, suddenly found his lap full of wriggling, panting, hysterically happy *othode*. He squealed and wrapped his arms around Fido, who was enthusiastically licking his face while wiggling ecstatically. It was all too sudden and too strange for Xara.

She uttered a helpless laugh and turned questioningly to Valkar.

"Sir, I know not by what fortuitous circumstance you came to snatch us from the very jaws—or, rather, hooves—of death, but for my part you have the undying gratitude of Xara of Ganatol," she said breathlessly.

The prince smiled, introduced himself, and explained that many of the scoutcraft of Shondakor were combing the Great Plains in search of her young companion in captivity and his Yathoon friend, and that he felt favored by the Lords of Gordrimator that it had been his good luck to be near enough to lend assistance to them in their peril. Then, sobering, he asked of Koja.

The girl's eyes fell. "Of Koja the Yathoon, and of his compatriot, Borak, I can tell you nothing," she said somberly. "They were in the wain, tethered near us . . . but, in the confusion, when the wagon struck a rock and came apart, and the guardrail to which we were fastened broke and freed us, I lost sight of the

two Yathoon. Indeed, I had only time enough to
snatch up the boy and jump free, before the wagon
overturned."

Her glorious eyes were somber.

"I never saw them again. And I greatly fear that
they went down beneath the slashing hooves of the
vanth. Even the horny armor wherewith Nature has
seen fit to clad the bodies of the Yathoon could not
have withstood for an instant of time those thundering hooves."

Valkar looked grim.

"That is indeed sorry news!" he sighed heavily.

And there was really nothing more to say.

From the moment he had first snatched Xara and
young Taran from the path of the stampeding *vanth*,
Valkar had paid little attention to the direction in
which Kadar had been flying the scoutcraft.

Kadar himself had paid no particular attention to
their direction, either. His primary objective was to
get the little ornithopter down close enough to the
surface of the prairie so that Valkar, dangling from
the bottom of the rope ladder, could bear the two
away to safety. And, once this had been accomplished,
he had lifted the craft with all haste—narrowly man-
aging to avoid striking his vessel against the upper
parts of the rocky hills.

These were, of course, the same hills whereupon
Koja and Borak had found a place of safety only
moments after the little Shondakorian scout soared
past overhead. But so thick was the blanket of dust
raised by the hooves of the stampeding herd that
neither Koja nor Borak so much as glimpsed the
ornithopter dart down, snatch up the princess and
the boy, and soar away with them clinging to the
bottom rungs of the swaying rope ladder.

And neither, of course, had the pair noticed the

dust-covered figures of the two Yathoon as they clambered up among the rocks of the hills.

Kadar had then simply let the craft fly itself while watching below as Taran and Xara and Valkar climbed the rope. Once he had assisted the exhausted, trembling princess and the excited boy to take their seats in the craft, he began to return his attention to flying the scoutcraft.

They had soared away from the terrible scene of disaster and carnage, as it happened, in the same direction as the *vanth* themselves were stampeding, which is to say due west. Borne along by a brisk tailwind, they had covered quite a distance by this time. But now Valkar determined that they should return to the site of the massacre in order to search for any signs of Koja and Borak.

This must be done first of all, before anything else.

For Valkar found it difficult to believe that the brave and loyal Koja had actually come to so ignominious an end as to be trampled to death by beasts.

Not until the last shred of hope was exhausted would he believe it.

And he dreaded having to tell Jandar and Darloona that Koja was dead . . .

"Turn us about and send us back to the place where the Horde was before the stampede," he directed Kadar. "If two could escape the holocaust, mayhap Koja and his comrade were equally lucky—"

Kadar leveled off and turned the scoutcraft about in a wide circle, returning the way they had first come. The stampede had long since passed, and naught but bare and beaten soil, trampled to dust beneath thousands of pounding hooves, was to be seen. That and, here and there, a fragment of splintered wood or crumpled metal. They could not even find any bodies.

And there was no sign of Koja or of Borak. These,

rescued by chance as we have already learned, had
long since ridden off with the hunters of the Kandar
to the distant encampment before Kadar returned to
the site of the massacre.

It is to Valkar's credit that he did not give up
easily. Bringing the little scout to a mooring place
in the hills, he descended with Kadar and the others
and searched the beaten earth for some sign or token,
however slight, as to the doom of Koja, finding absolutely nothing. At length he was forced to conclude
that Koja and his friend Borak had not been as lucky
as had Taran and Xara, and that the mighty Yathoon
and his comrade had met their end. There seemed no
other conclusion that was even remotely possible
under the circumstances. It was heavy news he must
bear back to Jandar and Darloona and Lukor and
all the other of Koja's friends . . .

But at least young Taran was alive and safe, and
Valkar knew that the Court of Shondakor would be
pleased that he had saved from certain death the
Princess of the Royal House of Ganatol. So, although
not a complete success, his mission had at least salvaged something from the debacle.

They would rest here on the plains this night, for
all were weary and worn out, and needed food and
sleep. With morning, Valkar would direct his craft
back to the rendezvous and rejoin the main force . . .
with the sad news that Koja of the Yathoon Horde
was no more.

He directed their flight on across the plains into
the south, following the path of the stampeding *vanth*.
At length they caught up to the mighty herd. Now
weary, their panic having faded, the *vanth* were dis-
persing in search of fresh meadow-grass and water.
It did not prove difficult to overtake and slay a fat
buck, which was quickly skinned and gutted. Kadar
built a fire and in no time juicy *vanth* steaks were

sizzling on a rudely improvised spit over a bed of crackling flames.

The meal was delicious, and doubly so for Xara of Ganatol, as it was the first food she had enjoyed in freedom for many months. After the pangs of hunger were assuaged, she and Valkar talked as night fell and the glorious panoply of the heavens blazed forth in all its splendor. Valkar was curious as to the nature of her mission to Shondakor and was alarmed to learn that the great Perushtarian Empire, which shared the coasts and waters of the broad inland sea of the Corund Laj with the kingdom of Ganatol, was making inroads against the freedom of her people.

The Perushtarians, a mercantile people, seldom given to warlike ways, had long been held in subjugation to the Sky Pirates, who had annually wrung from them a heavy tribute in wealth and slaves. Since the victory of the forces of Shondakor some two years or more before this time, which had resulted in the complete destruction of the City in the Clouds and had ended for all time the depredations of the Sky Pirates, it would seem that the Perushtarians had begun to expand their domain.

Valkar knew that this news would distress the rulers of Shondakor. For one thing, among Jandar's dearest and oldest friends was the gallant old sword-master, Lukor, a Ganatolian by birth, on whose behalf Jandar would surely mount some sort of assistance for the beleaguered city of Ganatol.

For another thing, there was the safety of Shondakor itself. Although the Golden City of the Ku Thad was probably the single most powerful of all of the cities of Callisto, Shondakor lay not far upriver from the center of the Perushtarian dominion. And, in any martial exercise, it would be but one city against four . . .

And those were unhealthy odds.

True, Shondakor had shared bonds of close alliance with the nearer of the four cities of the Bright Empire of Perushtar, the city of Soraba, whose Prince had joined with Shondakor, and with the free city of Tharkol in the great expedition to the Far Side of the Jungle Moon, where the combined forces of all three realms crushed forever the menace of the insidious Mind Wizards.

But in any real contest of arms, would Soraba continue to recognize her alliance with Shondakor, or would blood tell, and Perushtarian join with Perushtarian?

It was hard to guess what might happen under those circumstances.

But there was one thing that Prince Valkar knew for certain. And that was that the first advance warnings of warlike and imperial ambitions on the part of the Bright Empire had already been dangerously delayed. For Xara of Ganatol had been intercepted by warriors of the Yathoon before she had been able to bring the news to Jandar and Darloona, and ask for their help.

Thus Shondakor had, as yet, no intimations of the danger that impended from Perushtar.

And that news, Valkar grimly knew, was very, very important. No time must be wasted before Jandar and Darloona were apprised of these events. And it was of enormous and vital importance that Valkar and Xara bring the word to the attention of the Prince and Princess of the Golden City without any more delay . . .

Still, they were weary and needed their rest. Time enough, surely, to linger for a few hours of sleep, here amidst the endless plains. They could rise with dawn and be at the rendezvous point before midmorning . . .

And Xara was very beautiful.

And Valkar was only human.

The sweet, pure oval of her face filled his eyes. Her great eyes glowed like wet jewels. And the glory of the many-colored moons touched the rich sleekness of her silken hair with glimmering splendor. Valkar forgot to continue their conversation.

"I have not yet thanked you for saving my life," the Ganatolian girl murmured softly.

Her full, tender, moist lips were ever so slightly parted.

Valkar opened his mouth to murmur some polite reply—never afterwards could he quite recall what he had been about to say.

For, just at that precise moment, thirty Yathoon flung themselves into the circle of the firelight.

And, in the next instant, Valkar found himself fighting for his life.

15

Zothon the Mysterious

It was not actually Prince Valkar's fault. He had not really been careless or neglectful.

In the first place, Valkar had not fully realized exactly how far into the southlands they had flown. And he had no idea just how close they were to Sargol. Even if he had known, it is to be doubted that Valkar would have known enough about the Secret Valley, and how carefully it was watched and defended, to have been cognizant of his deadly danger.

Only in one respect had the gallant young Prince been careless. No woodsman, he had not realized just how far the light of an open fire can be seen on plains as broad and flat and unencumbered as those of Haratha.

And, of course, not being a Yathoon he could not possibly have known that this was that time of the Callistan year when the Clans of the Horde gather at Sargol for their games and ceremonies. At this period, every one of the gigantic, ferocious arthropods upon the entire planet were on the trek into the southlands; and thus it was that for the Shondakorians to have remained in the open about a blazing fire was the most dangerous thing they could have done.

He had no time to regret it now.

The ring of steel against steel filled the luminous silence of the night with harsh music. Already, in the first instant, Valkar had slain his nearest opponent with a reckless lunge. Now, as he parried the glittering blades of two others, he felt the warm pressure of Xara's body as the Ganatolian girl put her back to his own in order to defend his rear.

She had bent and lithely snatched up the sword let fall from the lax claws of him whom Valkar had first slain. Now she matched her steel against a tall, monstrously ugly Yathoon warrior, wishing she was armed with a smaller and more slender rapier rather than an ungainly whip-sword. But there was no hope for it.

Nature has not made the Yathoon particularly beautiful, save in a grimly utilitarian sort of way. But her opponent was singularly ugly even among his own kind, for a jagged scar snagged its way down the inhuman casque of his horny brow and had obliterated one of his bulging compound eyes, leaving it milkily opaque with blindness.

She dispatched him with a level thrust to the abdomen which took him by surprise. Since she was armed with a Yathoon blade, he had naturally expected her to employ the weapon after the Yathoon manner—which she did not.

Now, of course, Kadar and Taran had joined them, and the ringing of steel and the grunt of exertion and the harsh gasp of pain were the only sounds to be heard.

Even Fido the *othode* had joined in the fight, and his terrible jaws and burly weight had accounted for two of their attackers.

But it was soon over. Four humans and a single *othode* cannot hold at bay for long thirty towering, heavily armed arthropods. In tight-lipped silence,

Valkar threw down his sword and permitted his wrists to be bound.

Beside him, her head held stubbornly high, Xara of Ganatol did the like. The girl was crushed but refused to show it, and stubbornly blinked back the tears that stung her eyes.

"I am sorry, my Princess," muttered Valkar quietly in low tones.

Her voice was serene and untroubled as she replied: "*Va lu rokka,* my Prince." She smiled. But her heart was as a leaden weight within her breast. For it is cruel to have tasted so briefly of freedom after having for so long endured captivity—and to have the sweet cup dashed so soon from your lips.

"We will camp here and rejoin the caravan at dawn," the leader of the Yathoon said in his rasping, emotionless voice to an underling.

"What of the *othode*? Shall we slay it?" inquired the other, indicating Fido the *othode,* whom they had netted with their lassos. Growling and frothing, the *othode* pup was trying to bite his way through his bonds. They were of rawhide, however, which is proof against even the savage tusks and powerful jaws of an *othode.*

"Slay none," snapped the chieftain. "There has been enough slaying. We are on sacred ground." And he regarded with cold eyes the seven corpses which lay sprawled upon the turf. Valkar and his companions had acquitted themselves well.

They slept that night in the long grass, and with dawn they were tied to pack animals and rode into the south to rejoin the main caravan.

As for the skycraft, which had been anchored to the surface of the plains, it must be accounted among the casualties of the brief conflict.

For in the confusion of the swift battle, a random swordslash had severed its mooring cable, and it had drifted away upon the breeze, like some immense, ungainly kite escaped from its master.

This knowledge did nothing to improve Valkar's mood of grim despair.

For without the ornithopter, they were helpless to return to Shondakor, even were they somehow able to escape from their present state of captivity.

It was not very long before Prince Valkar learned that he and his companions had been taken prisoner by a scouting party of the great Zajjadar Clan, one of the mightiest and most numerous of the five which composed the Yathoon Horde.

The Zajjadar were, in effect, the Royal Clan of the Yathoon race, for the current Arkon (or Emperor) of the Yathoon Horde was himself a Zajjadar. He was above all Clan allegiance, however, and no longer actually commanded the Zajjadars; that position was held by a towering arthropod named Yazar, whom Valkar and the others had yet to encounter.

Nor did they particularly wish to do so.

These facts Valkar learned through furtive conversations with some of the other captives of the Zajjadars. There were many of these, for the Clan was renowned for its fearlessness in war, and had taken many captives during its long trek through the southern hemisphere of Callisto. Among them were bald, red-skinned Perushtarian traders, Shondakorian farmers and huntsmen, with their golden skin, green or amber eyes, and red manes, black-haired crimson Tharkolians, and one most peculiar young man whose unusual pigmentation and appearance piqued the curiosity of Valkar and his companions in misfortune.

His name was Zothon of Arzoma, and his people were known as the Laj-Thad. Since the same language is spoken and understood universally across the length and breadth of the Jungle Moon, Valkar of course

knew that this term meant "the People of the Sea."
But that was all that he knew about Zothon.

For he had never before heard of a place called
Arzoma, or of these Sea-People. Neither had he ever in
all of his wanderings encountered so strange and
unique a person as this Zothon.

For one thing, his hair was a stiff, bristling mane of
snow-white, and it resembled quills or very coarse
fibers rather than ordinary hair.

For another thing, Zothon's skin was of a greenish
hue, but of a shade so dark as to seem almost jet-black.
The contrast between his stark white mane and his
nearly ebon skin was startling and dramatic.

His eyes were every bit as unusual. They were of a
pale, jewel-bright shade resembling lavender, that is
the pupils were. But his eyes seemed to be almost entirely composed of pupil, and the whites were seldom
visible.

Like great sparkling sapphires were the peculiar
eyes of Zothon of the Sea-Folk. And Valkar soon became very curious about this strange personage.

As for his appearance, he was an odd, not unattrac-
tive, combination of lithe and sinewy strength together with a certain compactness of proportion so
flawlessly symmetrical that you did not think of him
as being smaller than the average human being, unless
and until you saw him standing next to an ordinary
man of Shondakor or Tharkol.

For one so slight, his physical strength, toughness,
and endurance were genuinely remarkable. Set to
toiling with the other slaves of the Zajjadars, he put
them all to shame by his extraordinary strength.

Valkar was intrigued by the mystery of his unknown
origin and homeland, but it was quite some time before, as chance would have it, he was chained to a
work detail next to the strange black man with the
startling white hair.

As soon as the first opportunity for them to converse

together without being observed presented itself, Valkar, as it were, seized it by the forelock.

"*Jaruga, notar*,"* he said in low tones.

"*Jaruga,* Valkar-*jan*," replied the other quietly. "For I trust that to be your name; at any rate, thus I have heard the young boy address you. I am Zothon the Arzomian, a Zetetikar of the Sea-Folk."

And here was another puzzle for Valkar to think about! For the word *zetetikar* means, simply, "seeker" or "searcher." However, Zothon used the word in such a way as to suggest that, among the people of his nation, it was a title or rank or, perhaps, a profession.

"What do you seek, for what do you search, O Zothon?" the Prince inquired.

"For many things, my Prince," replied the other. Then, with a slight smile, he remarked: "At the moment, for my freedom."

Then, as luck would have it, they were separated and assigned to different tasks, and Valkar did not for some time find another opportunity to exchange words with the mysterious black man with the white hair.

The Zajjadar moved south in rapid, day-long increments, pausing only at nightfall to erect their tents, eat the evening meal, and rest. Although Valkar remained alert and vigilant for the slightest chance to escape, none presented itself.

Nor did he again have the chance to speak to Zothon. None of the other captives to whom he spoke

---

* *Jaruga* is the simple word of greeting used throughout the nations of Callisto. A *notar* is a warrior, presumably one of noble rank, but whose actual rank is not known to the person addressing him. Another word for "warrior" is *chan*, which conveys the sense of "knight," and is used toward one known to be a noble or a gentleman. A *chanthan*, or "gentleman adventurer," is a landless member of the warrior class. It is, I suppose, only natural for a warlike society such as that of Thanator to have so many different words for the same basic thing, each expressing a different shade of meaning.

concerning the black man knew anything about him
or his unknown homeland. But it was the boy Taran
who noticed something even more peculiar and unique
regarding Zothon of Arzoma.

And that was that he had gills!

Now, as it happens, no true amphibians are known
to exist upon the Jungle Moon, although some of the
aquatic denizens, like the monstrous *groacks* that infest the waters of the Far Side of the planet, are able
to leave the depths for a brief time, in order to attack
their prey ashore.

But certainly no sea-dwelling race of intelligent
humanoids was known or even rumored to exist. Nor
did the legends and sagas with which Valkar was acquainted make any reference to a race of merfolk. So
this bit of chance discovery made Valkar even more
mystified than before.

But Taran was positive about his discovery. He did
not, of course, call them gills, but announced that once,
when he had toiled beside the black man at unloading
folded tents from one of the wains, the Arzomian had
gone stripped to the waist, and upon both sides of his
torso, situated parallel to his ribs, Taran had clearly
seen long, thin, pink-lipped openings in his flesh.

They were not scars, of this the boy was certain;
and neither were they open, unhealed wounds. Indeed, as the chest of Zothon rose and fell, straining
from his exertions, the long gill-slits had expanded
and contracted, rhythmically.

They could be nothing else but gills, and therefore
the true meaning of the name of his people, the Laj-
Thad, was to be defined literally. They were—*must be*
—dwellers beneath the sea.

This, of course, presented the Prince with yet another mystery to be solved. For only two bodies of water
large enough to be called seas are known to exist upon
the surface of Callisto, the Corund Laj at the north-

eastern border of the inhabited hemisphere of the planet, and the Sanmur Laj at the southwestern border.*

The greater sea of Corund Laj is ruled by the Perushtarians, whose cities are situated along its shores, with their capital, Grand Perushtar itself, upon a large island near the southern shores. And the trading and intercourse between the Perushtarian cities and the Golden City of the Ku Thad were such that, surely, if the depths of the sea had been inhabited by an intelligent aquatic race, everyone would know about it.

That left only the Sanmur Laj in the distant south as a good possible site for Zothon's city of Arzoma. The Lesser Sea was at a great distance from Shondakor and Tharkol and Ganatol, and was considered unexplored. No one had ever gone there, insofar as Prince Valkar was aware, for the plain and simple reason that there was nothing there that anyone would wish to visit. The sea was, as far as anyone knew, uninhabited and islandless, situated in the midst of a remote and hostile and uninhabited wilderness that bordered upon the far western terminus of the Plains of Haratha.

Could Zothon be from the Sanmur Laj, then, Valkar wondered. He supposed it was the most likely place. Unless, of course, there was another sea situated on the Far Side of Callisto, yet undiscovered by the Shondakorians. Only small portions of the Far Side had ever been explored, and the existence of a *third* sea was a distinct possibility . . .

So many questions, and so much that was mysterious!

And then it occurred to Valkar, almost whimsically,

* Corund Laj means "the Greater Sea," while Sanmur Laj means "The Lesser Sea."

that it was possible to put another construction upon
that curious word, Zetetikar, by which Zothon had referred to himself.

Besides the obvious literal meaning—seeker or searcher, or one who searches—the term could be interpreted
to mean "wanderer." *Zothon the Wanderer* . . .

Valkar smiled.

From whatever far, mysterious homeland he had
originally come, Zothon the Mysterious, with his
strange greenish black hide and stiff, startling mane of
bristling white hair, and weird sparkling sapphire
eyes, had certainly done a bit of "wandering"!

Day after day they came nearer with each long trek
to their unknown destination.

By day the horizons which lay ahead, to the ultimate
south, were blocked by a towering range of dark peaks
which could only be the famous and little-known
Black Mountains.

Nightly, the range blocked away the southern stars,
obliterated the glory of the many-colored moons behind weird, flickering, and luminous curtains of pallid
and ghostly light. That this phenomenon was essentially the same as the aurora borealis seen near the
pole of my own distant world I, Jandar, have no doubt.

For they were coming nearer and nearer to the
polar region of Thanator with every day's trek. At
dawn, thick frost mantled the long scarlet meadow
grass, which grew patchily here. By night they rolled
themselves in heavy furs for warmth.

Before long, snow crunched underfoot, and frozen
whiteness mantled the plains about them.

And the black wall of mountains rose before them,
blocking half the sky.

One afternoon, near dark, they entered a narrow
crevice in those tall and monolithic walls of soaring
rock.

All day the Zajjadar caravan had been threading a

path through rising hills, as through a winding laby-rinth.

Cold winds blew down the clefts between the soar-ing peaks, buffeting them unmercifully.

Valkar threw back his head and took one last look at the open and glorious and golden skies of his world before the mountains closed around them.

They were entering the most secret and closely guarded place of mystery upon this planet, he grimly knew.

And whether he would live to return to the outer world again, this he could not know.

Beside him the Ganatolian girl, Xara, shivered a little—but whether from the chill gusts of icy wind that screamed down the narrow pass or from the same inward trepidation that whispered within his own heart, he could not say.

His arm tightened about her slender shoulders. And, for a moment, her head drooped against his strong shoulder.

Then she gently disengaged herself and drew away.

And they passed into the Black Mountains and vanished from the knowledge of men.

BOOK FOUR

THE HIDDEN
VALLEY OF SARGOL

16

The Wall of Living Fire

For hours the vast numbers of the Zajjadar nomads streamed through the mountain pass, bound for their unknown destination.

Sheer walls of unscalable black rock soared to either hand to an incredible height, blotting out the moons.

The cold became numbing in its cruel intensity. Despite the heavy furs their captors had given them, Valkar and Xara and little Taran and the others felt the bitter wind. It pierced their flesh like the edge of a whetted knife.

And then, and quite suddenly, it became warmer. So warm, in fact, that before much longer, Valkar found that he had unconsciously opened the throat of his fur garments and tossed back upon his shoulders the thick fur hood that had shielded his head and neck from the wintry chill.

The air became steamy and redolent of an odor which Valkar could not quite name. It was like (he thought, wonderingly) the smell of a stone pavement when it bakes in the simmering heat of high summer.

But how could such heat be here in these frozen and glacier-encrusted mountains near the southern pole of Callisto?

Before very long, the first mystery was solved.

That peculiar acrid odor—like that of scorched stone—was explained when they rounded the next corner.

An immense valley lay before them, cupped in the bowl of the encircling mountains. Lush, warm, and fertile it was, with groves of flowering scarlet trees and running brooks. Toward the far wall of the girdling cliffs, a many-tiered structure stood—the first building of any kind Valkar had ever heard to result from the Yathoon—if, indeed, they were the builders, and not some lost, forgotten race of the dim prime.

Between the valley and the crevice that led to it blazed a moat of liquid fire. Like a river of leaping flame it effectively blocked the entrance to the Hidden Valley of Sargol.

Shielding his eyes from the scorching heat, Valkar peered more closely. A gummy black fluid, oily and viscous, leaked from an aperture in the cliffs and flowed through a deep channel in the rock to vanish at the other side of the entranceway to the Valley of Sargol. It was a seething mass of furious flames.

Now Valkar had heard of petroleum, for the engines which now drove the great ornithopters of Shondakor and the other of the Three Cities were fueled by that distillate. And he had seen pools of natural oil which sometimes came bubbling to the surface of the planet. If this oily seepage from the world's core was natural petroleum, which it seemed to be, then the mystery of the wall of living flame was easily explained.

And, from the lush fertility of the Valley, it was obvious that hot springs or underground volcanic fires were the source of the summery warmth in which Sargol basked. Who would ever have expected to find a fertile paradise here in the frozen southlands?

The crossing of the wall of living fire which was the

bastion of Sargol was easily effected by means of a wide drawbridge of heavy wood, entirely plated with tough metal, which was lowered into place by long chains.

The caravan, by this means, crossed the flaming moat unharmed. Once they were all safely on the far side of the river of fire, the drawbridge was raised once again.

And they were in Sargol—which obviously would not be an easy place to escape from, considering its unusual defenses.

One by one the great Clans of the Yathoon converged upon the Hidden Valley. When Valkar and Xara and the others were brought into the Valley as prisoners of the Zajjadars, the Angkang and Thoromé Clans had already arrived. A day after came the Haroob Clan, and then the Kandar.

The Valley was of broad extent, and areas were staked out for the use of the five great tribes. Slaves and captives pitched the tents after the immemorial fashion of the Horde, cookfires were lit, and the warriors mingled.

Valkar and the others, among the captives of the Zajjadar, saw little of this, busied with their tasks. Nor did the prince find a further opportunity to converse privately with Zothon the Arzomian.

When Koja, with Borak at his side, came riding across the metal bridge that spanned the fiery moat, evening was upon them. Under the glory of the many moons of Jupiter the Kandars pitched their tents and tethered their *thaptors* and the great *glymphs* which drew the heavy wains.

Koja, of course, had no reason to suspect that Taran and Xara were still alive. And he had no way of knowing that Prince Valkar of Shondakor, his lieutenant Kadar, and Fido the *othode* pup were anywhere within a hundred *korads* of the Hidden Valley.

That evening, together with the other Clan chiefs, he went with his retinue of warriors and chieftains to attend upon his Emperor. They strode up a stone-paved way toward the great marble citadel built against one wall of the Valley. By the light of the many-colored moons it could clearly be seen that this structure was a survival from some forgotten age, for Time had gnawed and worried at the fabric of the mighty walls, and all but obliterated the ornamental carvings which festooned the portals and the arches.

Within the vast, domed hall, guards were stationed and slaves scurried under the lash of the overseers to serve food and drink for the princes of the Horde.

Grim and silent was this feasting of the Yathoon lords, for they were a somber and humorless people, devoid of the gentler arts of civilization. Music and the dance were unknown to them, as were literature, drama, and poetry.

As *akka-komor,* or high chief of the Kandars, Koja occupied a position of great prestige, and was seated near the foot of the dais itself, in token of the honor his Clan enjoyed.

Upon the dais squatted the mighty Emperor, Kamchan, supreme overlord and Arkon of the Horde, surrounded by his slaves and servitors.

Among a race of mighty warriors, Kamchan was spectacular. His chitinous hide was scored with the scars of countless wounds from the innumerable duels and battles in which he had fought. His grim, expressionless visage was hideously disfigured. One knobbed brow-antenna had been sheared away in some long-ago battle. An axe blade had crumpled the corner of his mouth, and the wound had healed with a jagged scar that lent his face the likeness of a mirthless and horrible grin.

The Yathoon—clad as they are in a crablike shell of

armor—customarily wear no garments but a weapons belt and baldric. Kamchan, however, was covered with costly ornaments of precious metal, studded with numberless gems. His hideously scarred and towering body was one scintillant mass of dazzling gems.

He observed the surprising fact that Koja, long lost and long since believed slain, had somehow returned to his Clan and had now, obviously, risen to its highest rank. But he asked nothing about how these events had transpired, lest he lose dignity in so asking.

Eventually, however, the Arkon could contain himself no longer. While the thin, sour beer which the arthropods drink in lieu of the fine wines enjoyed by higher civilizations was served to the chiefs in bone goblets hollowed from the skulls of former enemies, he spoke up at last.

"We perceive, O Koja, that you have replaced the redoubtable Gamchan in the supremacy of the Kandars. How came this to be?" he inquired in somber, growling tones, harsh and heavy and rasping.

"O mighty Arkon, I was fortunate enough to best Gamchan, the former *akka-komor,* in a duel," said Koja expressionlessly. He then, at the urging of his Emperor, recounted the battle in some detail, which the Arkon pretended to enjoy hugely.

Actually, as things would have it, the Emperor of the Yathoon was severely displeased. A cruel and sadistic bully himself, he had been a crony of Gamchan of the Kandars, for like appeals to like, even among the emotionless insect-men. And he had never liked Koja, whose majestic and solemn dignity was natural and instinctive, and not feigned, and who possessed the finer and nobler traits of a brave and chivalric gentleman.

In another, these traits would have earned the scorn and the contempt of the Arkon, for he despised the softer sentiments of civilization and respected only indomitable courage and prowess. These, however, Koja also possessed, and the Arkon knew this well and from his own experience.

Upon more than one occasion the Arkon had faced Koja in the Arena during the Great Games, and had narrowly escaped his blade. He knew the Kandar for a formidable and courageous opponent, and, where in a nobler-hearted warrior than the Arkon Kamchan this would have won for Koja the admiration and respect of his Emperor, in the cruel heart of Kamchan it earned him but little. For he recognized in Koja, and always had, a potential rival for his throne.

Therefore, it did not in the slightest please the Emperor that Koja had returned from his wanderings to rejoin the Horde and had won for himself the chiefship of his Clan. He had thought Koja safely dead and buried years ago.

Koja concluded his brief and modest description of the battle in which he had bested and slain the former high chief of the Kandars, and the Arkon made no comment, merely giving a surly nod. Thereafter he ignored the new chief.

Koja returned to the tents of his Clan, which had been pitched against the edges of the forest that grew to the south side of the Arena, and composed himself for slumber.

He was well aware of the dislike the Arkon had always borne for him, and knew in his heart that by rising to the chiefship of the Kandars he had stepped into a new and perhaps dangerous prominence. As long as he had been merely a chieftain he had not really been important enough to be viewed by the malignant and cunning Emperor of the Horde as a foe and rival. Now everything was different.

Koja resolved to watch his step and to avoid giving affront to the Arkon Kamchan if he could possibly do so.

Otherwise, by crossing the river of living flame, he might find himself stepping out of the frying pan and into a hotter spot . . .

Night had fallen upon the Jungle Moon. The stars blazed, clear and brilliant, in the pure skies here near the pole.

One by one, the glorious and many-colored moons of Jupiter rose above the edges of the world to flood the snow-fields and, with their vivid hues, to gild the peaks of the Black Mountains with colored fire.

Sentinels from the Clans of the Horde stood watch over the narrow pass which led through the impassable wall of these mountains to the Sacred Valley hidden in its heart.

They stood, also, upon the cliffs and ramparts of the range, so as to give warning should an enemy force approach the heartland of the Yathoon race. Just because no such enemy had ever come into the frozen southlands was no reason for their vigilance to relax or their attention to become negligent.

Keen of sight and tireless were the sentinels of the Horde. However, even their black and jewel-like compound eyes, lidless as are the eyes of the insects they so closely resemble, did not detect the approach of a most unlikely foe.

For days now the burly and indefatigable *othode* had journeyed south across the interminable plains. By night he had rested, and by day his strong, bowed legs had carried him ever onward with no discernible lessening of his strength or of the unshaken resolve to find Taran and Koja and Fido, which burned in his mighty heart.

Only hunger and thirst could turn him aside from his undeviating descent into the south. When thirsty, he sought a stream or pool from which to quench his thirst; if his keen senses failed to detect the nearness of water, he then would track down one of the peculiar perambulating *jinko* trees whose bladderlike leaves stored fresh water.

And when his belly growled for food, he would turn from his path to hunt for game, to track it down and slay it, and then he would pause only as long as it took him to devour his kill.

And now Bozo the *othode* had come to the foot of the Black Mountains. The snow-fields had not been easy to cross, and neither had that crossing been comfortable. But nothing could deter the brave and loyal beast from his aim.

With his sensitive nostrils it was not particularly difficult for Bozo to track the Yathoon and their beasts through the maze of the foothills which rose before the soaring rampart of the Black Mountains. Nor was it difficult for him to slink furtively from shadow to shadow, eluding the watchers posted above the narrow pass.

But the wall of living flame he could not pass.

A dozen times he crept near to its brink, and each time the searing heat drove him whimpering back into the shadow of the boulders again.

At last, very near to dawn, the indomitable Bozo slunk away, retracing the pass to its mouth. At every twist and turning he sought another route through the unbroken wall of cliffs which rose to either side, seeking an alternate way that might lead him into the warm and fertile Valley he glimpsed beyond the impassible barrier of leaping flames.

It was not within the character of the Callistan hound to give up. If necessary, the *othode* would circle the entire range of mountains, seeking entry. Surely there was another opening in that clifflike wall of sheer black stone. Surely there was at least a chink in the stony ramparts through which he might wriggle.

Bozo would never give up, until death claimed him and his brave and loyal heart beat its last.

He paused to rest, there at the entrance to the pass, concealed in the deep shadows from the sentinels upon the heights.

He was footsore and weary, was Bozo. He was hungry and he suffered from the pangs of thirst.

But he was not beaten.

A day or two later, having traced the edges of the mountains in either direction for a great distance, Bozo returned to the mouth of the pass and threw himself down, panting, in the shade of the boulders.

There was nothing in his heart but the determination to somehow cross the river of flame.

And then it was that his ears pricked and his hackles rose.

For he heard the approach of mounted warriors, riding through the foothills toward the pass.

Bozo did not know that all of the members of the Yathoon Horde had already reached the Hidden Valley days before. He did not know that already the Great Games were underway, in which Koja and the others he sought were fighting for their lives.

Neither did he know the identity of the seven Yathoon warriors who came thus so tardily to the foot of the pass through the Black Mountains.

But he guessed that they knew a way across the river of fire.

And he determined to follow them.

He could not, of course, know that they were the last survivors of the decimated Garukh Clan.

He could not have recognized Fanga, the high chief, who rode among them: Fanga, who hated every Kandar upon Callisto—Fanga, who had not the slightest suspicion that his former captive, Koja, had been a Kandar and had now risen to the chiefship of the Clan that Fanga so loathed and hated.

Fanga and his warriors rode into the mouth of the pass.

And Bozo hesitated, whining, in the shadows.

Should he follow them, or seek again to find another route through the mountains?

17

The Trap

Dawn flared above the Hidden Valley of Sargol on the day after Koja had led the Kandars through the pass and into the heartland of his race.

It lit to flame the golden skies of Callisto, gleaming upon the walls of the Arena, the row upon row of Yathoon tents, and illuminating the tiered citadel of the Arkon.

With dawn, Koja broke his fast with his chieftains. Then, with Borak at his right hand, he and his chieftains rode across the Valley to the citadel which soared against its farthest wall.

There, in the great hall before the Arkon's throne, all of the high chiefs of the five Clans were assembled, with their chieftains.

With the Arkon and his retinue leading the way, the lords and princelings of the Horde descended by a secret stair behind the Arkon's throne into a mighty cavern hollowed deep within the living rock of the mountains.

They went in solemn silence. Only the clink of their weapons and accouterments and the tramp of many feet broke the sepulchral silence of this hallowed place.

They descended to look upon the precious and jealously guarded secret which their forefathers had hidden from the world for a thousand generations.

Deep within the cavern they entered into a chamber. It was capacious, that niche within the rock, and roofed with crystal so that the glory of the daylight fell in splendor upon rich carpets and silken cushions and the dainty furnishings wherewith the gaunt walls of stone and the rocky floor were rendered sumptuous.

There they looked upon the females of their race.

In all respects, the females of the Yathoon are identical to the males, but they are smaller and slimmer of build, and their mandibles are less developed and therefore lend them an aspect less ferocious and bestial than that of the males.

Their slim chitin-clad forms were naked and of a more mellow hue than the harsh coloring of the males. And, whereas the male Yathoon were naked but for their war harness, the bodies of the females blazed with a thousand gems.

In a deep, soft nest of meadow grasses reposed the larva. Like naked, glistening grubs they were, and repulsive to the human eye. But in the grave and melancholy gaze of the silent males they were incredibly beautiful. For from these larva would hatch the children of the Yathoon, which represented the future of their race.

As did the females.

In the Valley beyond, perhaps twenty thousand Yathoon warriors were encamped, the entirety of the race.

And here, within this cushioned holy of holies, *thirty-nine* females dwelt in sumptuous and silken luxury.

And this was the secret which the Yathoon concealed from the world. *Their race was dying.*

They looked long upon the sight of those precious

to them, then turned away and regained again the
open air.

That day the Horde conducted its business. Laws were
discussed, punishments bestowed, rewards given.

That night there was another feast.

The great hall of the citadel blazed with the light
of two hundred torches. At long low tables, seated
tailor-fashion upon cushions, the lords and princes of
the Horde feasted solemnly and conversed humor-
lessly.

Throughout the feast, and without seeming to do
so, the Arkon stole many furtive glances at his rival,
Koja.

Borak, seated upon Koja's right, was also under the
scrutiny of an old rival and enemy. For the Haroob
Clan were, of course, in Sargol for the annual Games,
and this was the Clan from whose chieftainship Borak
had been ousted by the jealous Gorpak and his cunning henchman, Hooka.

Throughout the meal, Gorpak had glowered across
the tables at the imperturbable Borak, muttering
surly comments about "traitors" and "renegades" in
harsh tones clearly meant to be overheard. It was only
proper for Borak to ignore them.

But the Arkon Kamchan noticed this exchange and
recognized Koja's chieftain as the former lord of the
Haroobs. The fact bore no obvious correlation to
the present situation, but, wily and cunning as he
was, the Arkon never let anything escape him and
filed this tidbit of information away in his cold,
Machiavellian brain.

You could never tell when a smoldering rivalry
between two warriors would be fanned to a blaze
which might consume a hated rival . . .

* * *

After the feast, the Arkon dismissed his chiefs but passed along word to Gorpak of the Haroobs to join him at moonset.

The two conversed for some time, circling around and around the central point, and parted near dawn in complete agreement.

With day, the Games began. Champions were selected from the five great tribal groupings to contest for the victory. And, although it was not customary for an *akka-komor* to compete against warriors of lesser rank or renown, Koja entered the lists as a common contestant.

Perhaps he felt that it was incumbent upon him to prove his prowess before the Kandars, that he might gain once again their loyalty and regard.

A famous champion, Koja competed throughout that day with the finest and most skillful warriors of the Five Clans, as often as not carrying off the victory. They fought with whip-swords, then with bows, followed by lassos, and finally with spears; afoot and mounted and in light chariots drawn by teams of matched *thaptors,* and the applause mounted with every victory that Koja won.

And with every victory won by his hated rival, the Arkon Kamchan's humor became more bitter and savage.

But, as for the lords and chieftains of the Horde, they admired the extraordinary skill and strength and prowess of the new Kandar princeling unreservedly. A warrior race born and bred, only a superior display of skill in the warlike arts could win their favor. And Koja triumphed during that long day, rapidly becoming once again one of the favorites of the Horde.

Borak as well, taking his cue from his chief, entered the lists and scored remarkably with bow and spear, to the envy and disgruntlement of the jealous Gorpak.

This fact did not escape the cold and watchful eyes of the Arkon.

And then there occurred one of those small accidents upon which the destiny of nations sometimes revolves.

When each contest was concluded, it was the task of each of the five Clans in turn to remove the corpses, broken weapons, and other debris, and to clean and smooth the fine sand with which the floor of the arena was covered. These tasks, of course, the warriors of each Clan gave over to their slaves and captives. And, as chance would have it, today it was the responsibility of the captives of the Zajjadars to repair the damage and remove the fallen. As Koja was retiring from the field, he happened to encounter the first of the slaves as they entered the Arena. Among them were none other than Prince Valkar, young Taran, Xara of Ganatol, and the lieutenant, Kadar. Koja stopped short in astonishment.

"Valkar of Shondakor, is it you?" he exclaimed. And in the next moment, Taran, crowing with joy, was hugging the towering form of his friend, while solemn Koja, somewhat dazedly, exchanged greetings with the Princess of Ganatol and Kadar.

And Gorpak of the Haroob Clan saw it all.

So did the Arkon Kamchan. That his hated rival had friends and comrades among the captives taken recently by the Zajjadar warriors was an interesting, a potentially valuable, fact. One of those little items of information which Kamchan liked to file away in his memory for later use . . .

That very night, as the chiefs of the Horde feasted in the citadel of the Arkon, there occurred that which caused events to move rapidly toward their destined, and sanguinary, conclusion.

It had greatly alarmed and disgruntled Gorpak to find Borak alive and among the chieftains of the

Kandars. From the position of obvious intimacy he shared with his high chief, Koja, it seemed very likely to Gorpak that Borak might prevail upon Koja to lend the strength and influence and prestige of the Kandars in an effort to dislodge Gorpak from his high place, in order that Borak might once again become the *akka-komor* of his Clan.

He had discovered, as well, that the Arkon was not unalterably opposed to the defeat or humiliation of Borak, since thereby might Koja also be made to fall from power. The two had discussed several means by which this might be effected; for the Haroob Clan were strong supporters of the Arkon Kamchan, or, at least, Gorpak and his hench-crony Hooka were.

An incident was arranged. Two of the Arkon's most powerful henchmen, Norga and Gorn—matchless warriors with great skill—were to rig a quarrel with Borak during the feast, and were to loudly demand satisfaction in blood. If Koja spoke up on behalf of his chieftain, then both Gorpak and Hooka were to announce that Borak—whom they would pretend to have just recognized—was *aharj,* that is, an outlaw and exile, and hence not under the protection of any Clan and fair game for the *duello.*

By this means, it was considered likely that everyone involved would gain their desired ends. Surely, Norga and Gorn would make short work of Borak, which would make Gorpak and Hooka rest easier. And Koja would have to stand by and swallow the humiliation of watching his comrade insulted, challenged, and slain before his eyes. Which would make him lose face before the other chieftains of the Kandars, lessening his prestige and thereby reducing his ability to remain a rival to the Arkon.

Things went according to this cunning plan. Borak, affronted, accepted the challenge. Koja, however, realizing that his friend stood little chance against two of the finest warriors of the entire Horde, spoke up to remind the council of chiefs of the Sacred Peace which invested all of the Valley of Sargol and made it a sanctuary in which duels, murders, and assassinations were strictly forbidden. The words were scarcely out of his mouth before Hooka and Gorpak rose to point out that Borak was an outlaw and hence under sentence of death anyway. And, in turn, according to their prearranged plan, the Arkon next rose to pronounce as his will that the outlaw Borak accept the challenge and fight to the death.

An endless moment of silence stretched taut in the vast room. Koja remained standing, staring levelly into the coldly malignant gaze of Kamchan. He saw—too late—the trap into which he had fallen. But he could not, in all conscience, stand idly by and watch his comrade butchered. The waiting became interminable. Then—

"I challenge your ruling, mighty Arkon," Koja said in a flat voice. The words, evenly spaced, fell one by one into the silence.

Kamchan blinked incredulously, a dawning wonder and delight growing within his cruel heart. Was it possible that Koja was challenging *him* to the *duello*? That would be the most satisfactory of all possible conclusions to this carefully arranged scene: a bully, stuffed full of overweening pride and lordly confidence in his oft-proven abilities, Kamchan deemed that he had little to fear from Koja.

"To challenge your Arkon's will," he grated harshly, inwardly gloating, "is to challenge your Arkon!"

Koja knew this very well. But, as an *akka-komor* of the Horde, it was his privilege to challenge the leader of the Horde to personal combat at any time. This was usually done only when one of the high chiefs of the Clans felt sufficiently confident of victory to risk unseating the Arkon, thereby to replace him. However, there was no way out of this now . . .

"I, Koja, *akka-komor of* the Kandars, challenge the

Arkon Kamchan to the *duello*," he said emotionlessly.

Kamchan instantly accepted. In the interval his wily, malicious brain had realized a way to utilize the valuable information he had learned only a little time before.

"As the challenged, it is my privilege to dictate the form and nature of the duel," he announced. And then he let fall the first thunderbolt he had been saving. *"It shall be in the form of a game of Darza, fought between Koja of the Kandars and myself, the Darza pieces to be represented by living men and women, of my selection."*

A murmur of consternation and surprise ran over the room, and there was a rustle of involuntary movement as the auditors of this astounding statement turned to stare in wonder at each other.

Koja nodded briefly, giving assent to the terms of the *duello*. The Arkon's passion for the game of Darza was widely known; so, too, was the fact that he was a great Darza master. But it could not be helped.

Then Kamchan let fall a second thunderbolt. He turned to Yazar, the high chief of the Zajjadars, and in a loud, ringing voice commanded him to select from among his captives four slaves whom he described, not knowing their names. The high chief of the Zajjadars acceded to his Arkon's request.

"These captives, together with the outlaw Borak, shall serve, O Koja, as your living Darza pieces," said Kamchan gloatingly.

Koja said nothing.

The captives who would fight in this game of living Callistan chess were none other than Prince Valkar, Princess Xara, Kadar of Shondakor, and little Taran.

And the game would be—*to the death.*

18

The Game of Darza Begins

Under the blazing skies of golden dawn the strangest
and most unusual game of Darza ever played in the
immeasurable ages which compose the history of the
Jungle Moon commenced.

"Darza" means, literally, "war-game," and is used
in the sense of "tourney," or "mock-battle." But now,
for the first time since the game was invented aeons
ago, it took on every aspect of a genuine tourney.

The sandy floor of the great Arena had already
been marked off into a Darza "field," which closely
resembles an earthly chessboard. Alternate squares of
dark- and light-colored sand formed a long rectangular
playing area composed of nine rows of seven squares
each.*

* You will find, in the Appendix to this book, a drawing of the
Darza field showing the disposition of the pieces, drawn up at
the beginning of the game. By this means my readers will be
able to follow each move in the ensuing game as it is made, if
they wish. I have also written up a description of each piece,
and the ways it can be moved, and the basic rules of the game.
I regret I do not have the space to discuss some of the tactics
of the game, for the literature on Darza is nearly as rich and as
complex as that of chess on our own world.

At either end of the gigantic chessboard, tall wooden thrones had been set up wherefrom Koja and Kamchan would overlook the field of play and control the movements of the players.

Now swords were solemnly struck against shields, the Yathoon equivalent of the braying of trumpets, and the living chessmen who would fight to the death for victory in this weirdest of all Darza games began to assemble.

They marched upon the field in two rows, and their garments were colored either Red or Black, representing the two sets of Darza pieces customarily used in the game.*

Kamchan and Koja took their positions as Prince on either throne, while their five players arranged themselves before each Prince in an open arrowhead formation. To Koja's right in the second row, as his Chieftain, Kadar was stationed, and to his left, Borak.

One row ahead of Kadar and to his left, Xara of Ganatol served as Bowman, while to Borak's right, in the same row, Valkar stood in position as Swordsman.

Spearheading the formation was young Taran, as Scout.

Koja was fully armed, befitting a Prince: he could move the entire length of the field if he chose, but only at right angles. Kadar and Borak, the Red Chieftains, were armed with sword, axe, and spear. They could move at right angles, too, but for only three squares each turn. As Bowman, Xara could move only on the diagonals, the length of the field if she wished. Valkar, the Swordsman, could move with exactly the same ease as a knight in chess—ahead two squares and over one square more, or ahead one square and over

_____
* Sometimes city colors are used, according to one's nation. In Shondakor, for instance, the game is played between Gold and Black, while in Tharkol the city color is Scarlet, in Soraba it is Purple, and in Ganatol it is White. Patriotism, I suppose.

two. He, of course, was armed only with sword and shield.

Taran, as Scout, could only move ahead one square at a time. And he bore neither weapons nor shield and was defenseless. But, if he reached "Prince's Row" —the last row on the field, currently occupied by Kamchan—he could become a Prince and would receive full weaponry. In effect, then, the Scout in Darza resembles the pawn in chess.

Koja's team were the Reds, and Kamchan's were the Blacks.

Kamchan had, perhaps maliciously, or perhaps because he knew how much they lusted for the death of Borak, positioned Hooka and Gorpak as his Chieftains, while for his Bowman and Swordsman he had chosen two renowned and skillful veteran fighters, Norga and Gorn. His Scout was a powerful arthropod called Orad.

And so this strangest of all games of Darza began . . .

It is customary to open with one's Bowman, moving him to the fifth square of the farthest row, so that he challenges the opposing Swordsman. Kamchan, however, advanced his Scout, Orad, so that he faced little Taran.

His motives for this unorthodox opening were extremely clever. This was no academic Darza match, but a battle to the death. In an ordinary game, the Red Prince would probably not scruple to sacrifice his Scout since, with his next move, he could take the Black Scout with his Bowman.

But here, of course, Koja would not care to risk the life of his young friend, for Orad was bigger and more powerful than the young boy, and in any struggle—even with bare hands—he could doubtless kill the youth. So Koja advanced his Swordsman, Valkar, two squares forward and one to the right.

As Valkar entered the square, Orad threw himself upon him, obviously determined to defend himself as best he could. A Yathoon, he was of course nearly twice as tall as the Shondakorian, with far greater reach of forelimbs, and the ability to leap high in the air—which is exactly what he did, kicking Valkar in the head as he sprang over him.

Not expecting the blow, Valkar did not block it and fell to his knees, shaking his head dizzily. Landing lightly beyond him, Orad whirled and seized his sword-arm, and strove to wrest the weapon from him. But Valkar struck out with the edge of his shield, catching Orad in the midsection, where the abdomen joined the thorax—a numbing blow. The stalk-legged giant staggered, and Valkar tore his sword-arm free and sank his steel into the heart of the Black Scout.

There was no applause. From his wooden throne in Prince's Row, the Arkon glowered grimly. Valkar stood, shaking his head to clear it and catching his breath, while slaves dragged the corpse of Orad from the field.

It then being Kamchan's move, he advanced his own Swordsman two rows ahead and one square to his right, so that he entered the square now occupied by Valkar. And a second pitched battle ensued, but this time between two equally armed warriors. Still, however, the advantage lay with the Black Swordsman, Gorn. The clash of steel, the shuffle of sandaled feet in the sand, the grunt and wheeze of effort were the only sounds that broke the stillness of the tense scene.

Xara felt stifled as if she could hardly breathe, and her heart thudded painfully against her ribs as the gallant Prince fought for his life against the towering Gorn, armed with his long, flexible whip-sword, which was nearly half again the length of Valkar's blade. The two circled, watching for an opening, while Gorn measured his singing needle-like blade against Valkar's long-sword. Each time he struck, he forced Valkar to

raise his left arm, catching the steel lash of the razory
blade upon his shield. The fourth time this happened,
Gorn kicked out with his long, double-jointed legs,
trying to give Valkar a crippling blow in the groin.

Valkar hastily dropped his shield, blocking the kick
—and then, before the Black Swordsman could bring
his whip-sword back into play to cut off his exposed
head, he risked all on a daring lunge *over* the top of
his shield.

It caught Gorn full in the breast, and, although
the tough chitin of his natural armor deflected the
stroke, it slashed a long and fairly deep furrow the
width of his thorax. Blood welled forth from the foot-
long wound. Gorn lurched to his knees and fell forward. Valkar bent and cut off his head.

The next move being Koja's, he commanded Valkar to
advance two rows and to occupy the square to the
right, which had been Gorn's original position. This,
in effect, put Kamchan, the Black Prince, in check,
for Valkar was only one move away from a duel with
the Arkon. Glaring and fuming, Kamchan was forced
to move to his own right one square, to be out of
Valkar's reach—which wasted him a move.

Koja now enjoyed a definite advantage, having
taken Kamchan's Scout and Swordsman, and, luckily,
having lost none of his own "pieces." As it was now
his turn to move, he pressed his advantage and advanced his Chieftain, Borak, three rows, so that he
stood directly facing the Black Chieftain, Hooka.
Borak's expressionless visage could not express the
grim satisfaction he doubtless felt, but the extreme
agitation of Hooka was obvious to all. The Black
Chieftain knew that Borak well remembered the trick
with the poison he had played, in order to drive Borak
into exile and to elevate Gorpak. And he quavered
inwardly, hoping against hope that Kamchan would
remove him from the reach of Borak's steel.

Kamchan, however, callously left Hooka where he was and unlimbered his Bowman, rightly determining that it was time he took the initiative again. He advanced his Bowman, Norga, to his left along the diagonal until, after two squares, he again menaced Koja's Scout, Taran. With the next move, Norga could easily slay the boy. Taran was pale but did not restrain himself from casting an appealing look in Koja's direction. Norga nocked his bow, and his cold, glittering eyes marked a spot on the boy's breast beneath which there beat his heart.

Koja had no alternative than to direct Taran to step forward one square, which placed him out of danger.

Then Kamchan, wishing he had placed another in the position, launched Hooka forward to engage Borak. The cunning and treacherous Hooka, as cowardly as he was clever, had no recourse but to attack. Sprinting forward, he leaped high, uttering a harsh, grating war-cry, and brought his whip-sword slashing down. But Borak caught it on his buckler and struck with his lance, narrowly missing Hooka's hurtling form. Landing lightly behind Borak, the Black Chieftain sprang forward, lashing out with his sword again. Borak imperturbably caught that blow on his shield as well, and struck out in turn. For long minutes the two warriors alternately lashed out with their whip-swords and blocked their opponent's return strokes.

Then Borak sprang into the air, leaping above Hooka. But, instead of striking downward between his legs with his whip-sword as he soared over the head of the other, he thrust with all the strength of his arm with his javelin, letting go of his shield. The thrust caught Hooka's shield—which was held above his head, for all the world like a veritable umbrella—square in the center-boss, and the impact drove the Black Chieftain to his knees.

Landing, Borak whirled and cast his gleaming lance.

It transfixed Hooka through the back as he knelt, pinning his corpse to the ground. In a ringing silence, Borak strode forward to take his proper position again, drawing his javelin forth from the dead Chieftain's flesh.

They dragged the corpse from the field, and over the heads of the combatants, Kamchan and Koja exchanged a long, eloquent look.

The move now belonged to Koja. He was clearly winning the game, for Kamchan had only one Chieftain left—Gorpak—and his Bowman, Norga, while Koja had preserved his full complement of human chesspieces untaken—which is to say, unslain.

But overconfidence has been the ruination of many a man, both in play and in war. Koja stared long and thoughtfully before making his move. He then advanced Xara, his Bowman, one square along the diagonal, to her right, so that she menaced Norga.

Kamchan growled under his breath, but he could not risk losing Norga. Then, cunningly, he instructed his Bowman to advance one square to his right, so that he now occupied Taran's original position as Scout. And now Norga menaced Koja's other Chieftain, Kadar, who, sweating and fuming at his enforced inaction thus far, still held his original position on the field.

Koja now had two possible moves that he could make, in order to extricate Kadar from his dangerous position. In an ordinary, or nonlethal, game of Darza, he might have permitted his Scout to take the Black Bowman by moving back into his original position; but in this case, to have done so would have meant pitting the unarmed Taran against the huge Norga. So Koja was forced to waste a move in altering Kadar's position; he moved his Chieftain two squares to the left, so that he was now stationed directly in front of Koja's throne.

And then Kamchan himself struck—and cruelly.

Against Taran!

For the boy now stood helpless and unarmed only five squares away, directly down the third row of the field. And Kamchan, as a Prince, could traverse as many rows as he wished. Flexing his jaw mandibles in a gloating and lustful grin—or the Yathoon equivalent thereof—the heavily armed Arkon strode down the row to where the boy stood with bare hands.

And time slowed down to a mere crawl for Koja, frozen on his high wooden throne above the field.

Xara cried out shrilly; Valkar cursed futilely from his position far up the field; Borak hefted his spear, glancing in question back to where his Prince sat motionless. Kadar unlimbered his own spear, waiting for Koja's word.

For Koja, it was an interminable, timeless moment of unbearable agony.

Of course, he could not simply sit there while his unarmed little friend was murdered in cold blood by Kamchan. To do so was unthinkable; rather would Koja himself step forward into the path of certain death.

But the Yathoon insectoids are coldly logical; for Koja to have directed Borak or any of the others against Kamchan would be to have broken the rules of the game, hence forfeiting it. *And that meant to forfeit the lives of Xara, Borak, Valkar, and Kadar, as well as Taran's and his own . . .*

Of course, there was nothing else to do. He could not merely sit there, while Kamchan ran the lad through. He would intervene, even if it meant that in the next moment of time the six of them must face a vengeful host of ferocious warriors, which is exactly what it did mean.

At least they would die with weapons in their hands.

Koja tensed, gripping the arms of his seat. He was about to rise and hurl his long, slender javelin at Kamchan . . . when Fate stepped in.

* * *

Kamchan advanced upon the half-naked boy, hefting his long, supple sword. He stood now directly before the square which Taran occupied. Taran, naturally, was very frightened, but he set his square young jaw and looked the towering Arkon straight in the eye, refusing to flinch or to break and run.

Kamchan struck—

Like lightning, Taran darted forward nimbly, ducking under the Arkon's blade, and ran between his legs!

Then he whirled—bent—caught Kamchan by the lower leg and pulled him off balance. Rasping a harsh oath, the Arkon fell on his face. The boy darted forth, snatched the war axe from Kamchan's harness, and drew back, hovering in a crouch, facing the giant arthropod, weighing the heavy axe in one capable young fist.

Probably at that moment everyone who partook in the scene forgot to breathe.

Koja, half-risen from his chair, froze again—and with a curt word arrested Borak and Valkar and the others in their tracks, for all of the Red players had half-started forward instinctively to the boy's aid.

Is it possible that it might not be needed?

That one thought rang through the minds of Valkar, Koja, and the others at the same instant.

Kamchan, having regained his feet, glared furiously down at the nimble boy. Then, rasping an oath, he slashed out again with the whip-sword—a vicious blow that would probably have cut the half-naked boy in two had it landed.

But it did not land! Lithe as a dancer, Taran wove to one side, avoiding the blow.

The boy's mind raced, thoughts tumbling through his head rapidly. His heart was pounding and his breath came in short, panting gasps, but his head was clear and cool as he weighed possibility against possibility.

The towering arthropod, with his long gaunt arms, and with the length of the whip-sword to boot, had a reach that enormously outmeasured Taran's. So there was no way the boy could close with his opponent and use the axe as it was meant to be used.

Instead, he flung it.

For all the world like an Apache hurling a tomahawk, the boy swung back his arm and let the axe fly. The heavy blade flashed wickedly in mid-air as it caught the glare of daylight, spinning end over end.

But Taran knew little of the art of axe-throwing, wherein precise balance and timing are all-important.

Therefore, the axe whipped end over end one time too many, and it was only the *flat of the handle* which caught Kamchan, and not the blade.

Still, the axe was forged of heavy steel, and the blow struck with staggering impact. It caught Kamchan upon the forelimb—about where the wrist would be on a human arm—and the blow was numbing.

Kamchan croaked with the shock of the blow, and his whip-sword fell from his suddenly strengthless grasp to thud against the sand.

And now both Taran and Kamchan were disarmed. But only for the moment, for Kamchan had only to draw forth his sword or spear.

And Taran had only his bare hands with which to fight.

Then it was that the unexpected happened—and a more timely diversion even Taran himself could not have hoped for.

19

Unexpected Interruptions

For it was at that precise moment that the self-control of Gorpak *broke*.

The cowardly and treacherous chief of the Haroobs had stood there on the field all morning, trembling in abject terror of having to do battle with Borak, his dreaded blood-enemy.

The interminable chessgame had sapped his ability to stand and wait for doom. Finally, his nerve broke and he went momentarily mad. Uttering a harsh, maniacal scream, he flung down his shield and swung his whip-sword in a frenzied and cowardly blow against the back of his nearest opponent, which happened to be Valkar.

The Prince, of course, had turned his back on Gorpak to watch the unequal but incredibly daring battle which little Taran had been waging with the dreaded warlord of the Horde. The thought that the Haroob chief would try to sword him down from behind had never so much as entered Valkar's mind.

The blow caught him across the arm and back and shoulder. He cried out and sagged forward upon his face. Blood spurted from the open wound, drenching the sand of the square in which he had fallen.

Suddenly—as we Earthlings would say—all hell broke loose.

Gorpak drew his arm back for another blow. But it never landed. For Borak the Yathoon, seeing his hated enemy's cowardly blow fell the Prince from behind, sprang across the field and leaped upon him like a tiger. With one savage stroke of his sword he cleft the villainous Gorpak to the jaws, splitting his head in two.

Xara had whirled when Valkar was struck down. Lifting her bow, she had been about to put an arrow through the Black Chieftain.

At that moment, Norga, the Black Bowman, who stood only two squares from her position, lifted his own bow to slay the girl.

But that arrow never flew, for out of nowhere there was launched a living thunderbolt of purple fur. From the shadow of the trees, from which point of vantage he had lain patiently in concealment all this while, watching the deadly game of Darza, a mighty *othode* sprang and launched himself through space upon the Bowman.

Froglike mouth gaping wide, the iron jaws of the immense beast clamped down upon the head of Norga, and closed like a powerful vise, ripping his face away. *Bozo the* othode *had reached his friends at last.*

No one was ever to know by what means the faithful and loyal-hearted beast had entered the Hidden Valley of Sargol.

Perhaps he had slunk across the iron drawbridge in the train of one or another of the Clan caravans, when they came one by one into the Valley. Or it may have been that his matchless instincts as a hunter had enabled the tireless *othode* to find a pathway through the ring of mountains that encircled Sargol.

Whatever the means whereby he had entered Sargol, Bozo could hardly have entered the bloody game at a better time. Now he raised his gory and dripping jaws from the corpse of Norga and lifted his deep-chested voice in a baying call.

From the pens of the Zajjadar some distance away there arose a mournful howl. A moment later wood shattered, and the gaunt form of Fido the *othode* came awkwardly gallumphing across the Darza field, trailing a broken length of chain. The two beasts sniffed each other warily, then Bozo, like an anxious parent, began licking his pup as if to make certain that he was unharmed. Fido wriggled ecstatically.

While the beasts cavorted, the humans and the arthropods stood in grim confrontation, measuring each other with their eyes, weapons drawn and brandished nakedly in the daylight.

Kamchan shakenly recovered his shattered composure. Stooping, he snatched up the whip-sword young Taran had knocked out of his hand, and, without deigning to so much as glance at the young boy who had come so perilously close to besting him in the *duello,* he stalked with chilly composure back to his own end of the field.

The only living persons on that field were Koja and the five members of his team. All of Kamchan's warriors of the Black had been slain.

"I declare that Koja's players have forfeited the game," said Kamchan in loud tones—once he was clear and out of reach. "The penalty is, of course, death. Archers, strike them down!"

The bowmen, who stood along the forefront of the throng gathered to view the strangest game of Darza ever played, there to keep order and to see that the game was played according to the rules, now stepped forward at their Arkon's command, raising their bows.

And lowered them, hesitantly, uncertainly.

For this was against the rules.

Again Kamchan in a loud voice commanded them to

perform their duty. But this time a tall, plumed warrior stepped forth. It was Gorja, high chief of the Angkang Clan.

"One moment, my Arkon," said this personage in
cool, level tones.

"Why this interruption, O Gorja?" snarled Kamchan.

Imperturbably, the Angkang chief turned to address the other chiefs of his rank, the leaders of the
Horde—excluding, for the moment, Koja himself.

"I am no more expert in the game of Darza than
are many here," said Gorja, "but to my eye it does
not seem that the Reds forfeited the game, for it had
already been forfeited by the Blacks."

"What do you mean?" Kamchan demanded, glowering.

"My meaning is that when Gorpak the Haroob
struck down the Red Swordsman there"—and he
pointed to the fallen Valkar, who lay with his head
pillowed on the lap of Xara while the Ganatolian girl
strove to stanch his dreadful wounds—"that Gorpak
struck out of turn. It was not the Blacks' turn to move.
By moving, he broke the rules of Darza, and it seems
to my judgment that the game is forfeited and that the
victory must go to the Reds."

Kamchan literally foamed at the mouth in maniacal
rage and fury. Then, mastering himself, he said:

"And I suppose the Reds did not forfeit the game by
employing their beast to strike down the Black Bowman?" he sneered, nodding to where the faceless corpse
of Norga lay sprawled in a pool of reeking gore.

"Who has established that the beast belongs to the
Reds?" replied Gorja calmly. "It seems to me that the
appearance of the *othode* upon the field was as much
a surprise to the Reds as it was to the unfortunate
Norga."

Kamchan could answer only with a strangled grunt,

so choleric was the emotion which gripped him by the throat.

"In such an event as this," suggested Gorja equably, "it seems only fair that the opinions of the chiefs of the Horde be consulted, excluding only Koja of the Kandars, since his own fate is involved. And, of course, excluding also the Haroobs, who have no chief, since Gorpak has been slain."

That left only three other Clans whose leaders were to be consulted, the Angkang, the Zajjadar, and the Thoromé. And the Zajjadar Clan, of course, was the Clan to which Kamchan had originally belonged.

The vote was quickly taken.

Erza of the Thoromés gave as his opinion that the Blacks had forfeited the victory when Gorpak treacherously struck out of turn, and declared the Reds to be the winners.

Yazar of the Zajjadars, however, believed that the Reds had lost when they employed Bozo the *othode*. His position was precisely contrary to the facts; however, he proved adamant.

Gorja of the Angkangs announced that, in his opinion, the Blacks had cheated and had forfeited the victory to the Reds.

Then it was that, entirely unexpected, a fourth voice spoke up:

"I, Fanga of the Garukhs, declare with Yazar that the Reds have forfeited their victory!"

Koja and the others stared about with amazement. For, insofar as they had known, Fanga, their former captor, had been trampled to death beneath the thundering hooves of the stampeding *vanth*. How, then, came he here alive?

However he had escaped the almost certain doom, there he stood, with a half a dozen of his warriors ranged about him. And he could not possibly have entered the Sargol at a less opportune time—from the viewpoint of Koja and the others, that is. For there were now *four* chiefs to vote on the forfeiture, and Fanga's malice toward his former captive, who had since risen to the highest position among the despised and hated Kandars, was so vehement that he had sided instinctively with Koja's enemies.

And the vote stood evenly divided, two for the Reds and two for the Blacks. It was a stalemate.

Which could only be broken in one way.

Koja stepped forward and threw down his sword in the immemorial challenge.

"Let us resolve this dispute by continuing the contest in the form of hand-to-hand combat between the Arkon and myself," he said in clear, ringing tones, "since the farce of the game of Darza has been accidentally ended and cannot be resumed. Decide, O Chiefs!"

There was only one decision possible, and it was soon made.

Valkar, now unconscious and seriously injured, was tenderly borne from the Arena by Kadar and Xara and Taran, accompanied by the two *othodes*.

There are no physicians among the Yathoon Horde, for such is their callous and inhuman indifference to suffering that an injured warrior, even of their own kind, is left to die untended. But among the captives of the Zajjadars there was a fat Soraban who had been a doctor of medicine in his native city by the sea, and Koja directed that he be requested to attend the wounded prince.

Zothon the Arzomian hurried off to fetch this individual, whose name was Yetzl. The fat, fussy little red man examined Valkar's wounds and found them serious but not, with luck, fatal. Gorpak's blow had been across Valkar's back and shoulders, which were unprotected by mail. However, the thick, tough leather of Valkar's wide baldric and the criss-cross straps of his war harness had deterred the stroke just enough to prevent it from crippling the Shondakorian. Very quickly the bleeding was stanched and the cut cleansed and treated with healing herbs and salves, and sewn shut with many stitches.

Valkar was taken into Koja's own tent, with Xara and Doctor Yetzl to attend to his needs.

The corpses of Gorpak and the other dead were now removed from the field, and the markings of the Darza gaming squares and rows were obliterated. The fine sand was raked smooth, and Koja and Kamchan faced each other, swords in hand.

Koja was calmly aware that this would probably be the single most important battle that he had ever fought, or would ever fight. For if he was defeated by Kamchan, it meant not only his own death but the deaths of them all—Xara, Valkar, Taran, Kadar, and undoubtedly the two burly *othodes,* as well.

But if. *he* defeated Kamchan, he would become the uncontested Arkon of the Horde, and it was well within the scope of his powers to set his friends free and even to escort them back to Shondakor the Golden.

Koja was a matchless swordsman and a great champion. But Kamchan was accounted the greatest fighting man in all of the Yathoon Horde, and had defeated and slain dozens of warriors who had striven to replace him.

If Koja won, or if he fell, it was *va lu rokka*—"destined." And he felt no fear, only a firm and unshaken determination to slay the tyrant so that his friends might go free. For their lives were in his hands, and the lives of one's friends are a heavy burden for any warrior to bear.

The two combatants were armed with spear, whipsword, war axe, and a long stiletto or poignard. Each bore a small round buckler of light weight, fashioned from tough, lacquered leather tightly stretched over a wicker frame, securely strapped to his left forelimb. Other than this, they were naked.

Kamchan struck first with his spear, which he hurled point-blank at his opponent, hoping to take him off guard. But Koja stood his ground without flinching, merely batting the hurtling shaft aside with his own spear.

Then he advanced upon Kamchan, jabbing with his spear, forcing the other to give ground. They circled each other until, with a lucky stroke, Kamchan caught the wooden shaft of Koja's spear with a whistling stroke of his whip-sword and snapped it in half.

Koja flung the butt of the spear in Kamchan's face. And when he lifted his shield to catch and deflect the spear butt, Koja sprang upon him, aiming a deadly stroke with his long, whipping sword.

However, it did not land, for with one remarkable flexion of his double-jointed, insectlike legs, Kamchan leaped backward and avoided the slashing stroke.

Then Koja ran forward and sprang directly over Kamchan's head, striking downward with his whip-sword as he soared above his foe. Kamchan caught the stroke upon his shield, but it was deeply slashed—cut almost through by the stinging fury of Koja's stroke.

Coming lightly to earth a few paces behind Kamchan, Koja leaped upon him and hurled a rain of furious strokes. Some Kamchan deflected with his own blade, others fell upon his buckler, which was coming apart by now. Kamchan reeled dazedly beneath the storm of steel: never in all his days, it seemed to the Arkon, had he faced so tireless or indomitable an opponent.

Suddenly, he sprang forward to close with Koja, striking out, as he did so, with his war axe, which Koja caught upon his shield. So terrific was the force of Kamchan's blow, however, that it clove entirely through Koja's buckler and wounded his forearm slightly.

Koja untied and cast away the ruined shield, and now for an interminable time the two fought with sword alone. The chiming of steel upon steel—war's cold, ferocious music—filled the tense silence which was otherwise broken only by the shuffle of their feet in the dry sand and the hoarse panting of their breathing.

Then Kamchan aimed a savage slash at Koja's face, but it was a ruse. For he deflected the weapon from its path at the last possible moment and caught Koja across the left shoulder—a crippling blow. But the "shoulder" of a Yathoon's arm is shielded by Nature with a heavy cusp of chitinous armor that covers the joint. This was cut through, but the blade did not sink deep into the shoulder itself, quite possibly crippling Koja for life, because Koja permitted himself to roll with the blow while his natural covering of chitin absorbed the worst punishment of the stroke.

Nevertheless, his arm went numb and strengthless, and blood trickled down the paralyzed limb.

Scenting the heady aroma of victory, Kamchan now moved in for an attack of such savagery and utter ferocity that Koja could only fall back from it, helpless, with just his sword-arm to defend himself.

Then Koja tripped and fell backward, sprawling in the sand, and as he did so, he lost his sword. It whirled away, thudding to the floor of the Arena some dozen feet away.

Kamchan would have smiled then, a cold, gloating, cruel smile, but Nature did not design the visage of her most savage children with the ability to smile. Eyes gleaming with cold blood-lust, he stood over the fallen Koja and raised his whip-sword in both hands, to bring it down in one great slashing blow that would end the battle and the life of Koja.

As he raised his sword he also raised his eyes.

And something he saw in the skies caused him to gape incredulously. His timing faltered, his sword wavered.

And Koja, from the ground, seized this momentary diversion. Snatching his stiletto from its scabbard on his harness, he struck upward, sinking the needle of hard steel to the hilt in Kamchan's abdomen.

A hoarse cry roared from twenty thousand throats as the Arkon, already dead, wavered drunkenly on his feet, then fell over, and lay face down in the dry sand. From his belly a pool of scarlet gore spread, and the sand sucked in the moisture of his heart's blood.

Koja got to his feet, bent, and severed the head of Kamchan completely from his shoulders.

Koja—Arkon of the Horde!

Chiefs and chieftains and warriors stalked to where he stood, to kneel before him, offering their swords, giving their new Arkon their loyalty and allegiance.

Koja solemnly accepted their vows and permitted them to place upon his head the triple-plumed head-dress of the Arkonate.

But from time to time he raised his head from where he stood surrounded by groveling chieftains and warriors, to stare up into the sky, even as Kamchan had done for one brief—and ultimately fatal—instant.

Staring up to where the lone ornithopter, the *Shondakor*, floated weightlessly above the Hidden Valley of Sargol.

And looking directly into the smiling eyes and re-lieved and friendly features of Jandar of Callisto—the man who had taught him the meaning, and the value, of friendship and of love.

20

Escape from Sargol

I was enormously relieved to recognize Koja among the kneeling chiefs and warriors of the Horde. Although I did not, at that time, have any knowledge of how recent events had carried him to this situation, it was obvious that he was in no danger from the Hordesmen. Indeed, from the way they knelt in homage before him, I realized that he had somehow achieved a position of great prominence among his fellow Yathoon.

Satisfying myself that all was well with Koja and the others, I directed my pilot to remove the airship from the vicinity of the Valley, lest it be seen by the sentinels and the alarm be raised, causing consternation to the assembled Horde and, just possibly, putting my friends in danger once again.

We slept that night aboard our craft, floating above the snowfields. And, with dawn, as I had rather expected he would do, Koja came riding forth down the pass through the mountains, ostensibly to go hunting.

With him were Borak, whom I remembered from our former meeting, and little Taran, and Fido and Bozo, who were both mightily pleased to see me again, and my officer, Kadar. We conversed for two hours, there in the hills, the sentinels having been withdrawn by the express command of the new Arkon.

For the better part of a month, my squadron and I had combed the great prairie in all directions, gradually approaching the Black Mountains. When Valkar's scoutcraft had not returned to the rendezvous point at the time previously arranged, we concentrated our attention upon that portion of the plains that had been assigned to him and Kadar.

Eventually we found the scoutcraft itself, drifting idly on the wind, empty and abandoned. The mooring cable had been severed, we noticed, and to my eye the cut most closely resembled that made by a whip-sword.

And that meant the Yathoon were somehow involved in this new disappearance.

First, Taran and Koja and Fido and Bozo had vanished into the southlands. And now those same southlands seemed to have swallowed up Valkar and his lieutenant.

As the Yathoon insectoids were the undisputed masters of the southern hemisphere, it did not take us long to guess the culprit. Thenceforward we directed our vigilance to the regions dominated by the Yathoon, known to infest the Black Mountains.

Towing the abandoned scoutcraft behind us, we directed the *Shondakor* above what turned out to be the Hidden Valley of Sargol—and just in time, it seems, for our appearance in the skies to distract the murderous attention of the victorious Kamchan for one precious instant.

It was with vast relief and satisfaction that we discovered our lost friends alive and relatively unharmed. Koja's injuries proved superficial, while Valkar's were more serious. But none of the others had suffered very much from their adventure, and even the two *othodes* were unscathed.

During our conversation, each of my friends related the story of his adventures to me—the which I have written down in this volume, more or less as they were narrated to me. I was saddened to learn that Prince Valkar, my wife's cousin, was seriously injured, and I was also alarmed and distressed to learn that the Bright Empire was threatening the peace and security of Ganatol, one of our neighbors to the north.

There had never been aught but peaceful conditions between Shondakor and Ganatol, for we were too distant from one another for war to ever have been particularly desirable or even practical, had it ever been desired. An occasional merchant caravan, a bit of seasonal trade, sometimes a friendly exchange of greetings or embassies—little more.

But the opportunity to form a firm alliance with our neighbor to the north was exceptionally attractive, and I determined to pursue it upon my return.

Various difficulties presented themselves as obstacles to the freedom of my friends and of the new acquaintances they had made while in Yathoon captivity. For one thing, all except Koja and Borak were captives of the Zajjadar Clan, and were Koja to free them by mere command would be for him to insult and anger the powerful Clan, endangering his own position in the Horde. I suggested that Shondakor ransom them; since actual wealth is of no particular use or value to the Yathoon barbarians, an exchange of trinkets was arranged. The Yathoon hoard in their troves much the same sort of bright, glittery trash that may be found in a jackdaw's nest. Beads and mirrors and glass jewelry and trinkets are to them as desirable as treasure. Koja promised to arrange the exchange as surreptitiously as he could, for to be seen actively participating in the freeing of human captives might be extremely detrimental to him in his new capacity as Arkon.

After the departure of my friends—the two *othodes* we of course kept with us, as they were of no value or interest, even to the Zajjadars—I flew the *Shondakor*

back north into the grasslands to the place where Koja
and Taran and Fido had left the *Lankar-jan* tethered
to the upper branches of a tall stand of *borath* trees.

We found the little scoutcraft intact and still securely anchored to the treetops, apparently none the
worse for wear. Towing it behind us, we returned to
the Black Mountains to await Koja's signal.

Later that day, Borak emerged from the pass
through the mountains, with two trusted Yathoon warriors, to receive our store of gewgaws. My officers and I
had stripped ourselves of every ornament and bright
scrap of decoration we could find on our persons or
among the fittings of the two ornithopters, including
some valuable optical instruments and navigational
devices which we presumed might be rare and curious
oddities to the simple arthropods.

That evening Koja himself came down into the
hills, escorting Taran and Kadar and others. Prince
Valkar, sleeping easily under the influence of drugs ad-
ministered by the fussy little Soraban physician, was
borne on a litter. With him were Xara of Ganatol,
whom I was pleased to meet, and that curious personage introduced to me as Zothon of Arzoma, the repre-
sentative of a race I had never previously encountered
during all my wanderings across the broad face of
Thanator the Jungle Moon. These five former captives were now free, ransomed by the glittering trash
we had scavenged; free, too, was Doctor Yetzl, who
was still attending to Valkar.

Koja solemnly informed me that he would not be
returning to Shondakor, at least not at once. First he
must consolidate his position as Emperor of the Yathoon Horde. And it was also his avowed intention to
introduce certain novel concepts into the ancient and
immemorial traditions of the Yathoon race.

During his years with us in Shondakor, my friend
Koja had learned the value of some of the softer sentiments normally unknown to his emotionless kind, and,

even when known, regarded with revulsion and distrust as ennervating and effete.

The first thing he intended was an innovation in the nature of the Great Games themselves. Since the Yathoon race was gradually dying out—a secret which he confided to me in solemn confidence—it should not be difficult to persuade his princelings and chieftains to abandon the bloody games, hitherto fought to the death, in favor of contests of athletic excellence and martial skill. This innovation was rather like banning warfare in favor of something like the Olympic Games, but Koja felt confident that he could do it.

The Yathoon are coldly emotionless; reason and logic appeal to them where vehement passions cannot sway them. Simply to point out that irreplaceable lives are lost from a dwindling race when the Games are fought to the death should, he thought, suffice to convince his lords of the folly of the ancient practice. It's only real purpose, after all, was to make certain that the healthiest and most superior specimens of male Yathoon adulthood were permitted to lie with the females and breed the next generation. Athletic contests should weed out the sickly or unfit as certainly as pitched battles, and without further decimating the strength of the Horde.

At this time Koja also introduced to me his mate, a slender and elegant female named Nourya. His prize for excellence in the Games, and for winning the throne by the defeat of Kamchan, was the right to breed with Nourya for a season.

Never having been introduced to a Yathoon female socially before—never having even *seen* one, come to think of it!—I was fascinated to meet this first member of Koja's harem. As for Nourya, she seemed quite unexcited or nervous at meeting a human male, and greeted me calmly, as if it were an everyday occurrence for her to be introduced to a Prince of Shondakor.

The emotionlessness of the Yathoon is something

I will never quite come to understand or feel comfortable with.

Among the other innovations that Koja planned to begin introducing to his subjects was that of parenthood. When the larva laid by his mate hatched, Koja intended raising the cadet in full acknowledgment of his paternity. This would doubtless be viewed with mixed emotions by his subjects, who were about the most hidebound band of strict conservatives imaginable, and it might even scandalize them. But Koja was of the opinion that, in so doing, he would not seriously jeopardize his claim to the throne or his authority among the Clans.

He was curious to learn if this novelty in child-rearing would inculcate in the as-yet-unborn cadet something resembling the normal feelings of filial devotion common to human children. He rather suspected that it would.

I think he was also curious to find out if he himself could feel love for his own offspring. I rather suspect he will . . .

And, then, something would have to be done about the many slaves held captive by the various Clans. Having been a slave himself to the Garukhs, Koja naturally did not feel that he would stand idly by and watch the misery of the human captives held by the Horde—separated from their wives or families and far from the cities of their birth, hopeless possessions of a soulless and unfeeling and very alien race.

The freeing of the slaves, however, must be done gradually so as not to disrupt the traditions of the Yathoon with unnatural haste. But the paying of ransom for the lives of captives was not unknown to the arthropods, and Koja believed that he could gradually, in slow stages, encourage representatives of Shondakor and Tharkol and Soraba and the other cities of Callisto to attempt the ransom of their own people.

I promised to discuss this with the rulers of the neighboring cities and to arrange for the exchange of prisoners.

Koja also hoped to introduce reading and writing to the Yathoon, and to discourage the *duello,* and to begin something like a code of laws to govern in the place of ancient traditions. But all of these things would require time and patience and tactful persuasion—if inaugurated too swiftly, or all at once, the Yathoon Hordesmen would doubtless balk and Koja himself might be unseated. But he firmly intended to initiate these more civilized measures when he felt that the time was right.

Now that Koja had related to me all of his recent adventures, I was curious to learn how he was conducting himself as Arkon of the Horde.

The very first thing he had done, Koja informed me, was to set his comrade Borak in place as the new high chief of the Haroob Clan. As Borak had formerly held that position, and was himself raised among the Haroobs from the time he was a mere cadet, this afforded no real problem. And, of course, Borak had slain Gorpak, the former high chief, in man-to-man battle, which made his elevation to the princely office in accordance with the oldest Yathoon traditions.

The only one who might have objected strenuously to his attaining the chiefship would have been the wily and treacherous Hooka. But since Hooka had been slain in the famous game of live Darza—and I was genuinely sorry not to have been a witness to that most amazing chess game ever played on Callisto, I assure you!—there was no one left to raise his voice against the chiefship of Borak.

In fact, the Haroobs were by this time heartily sick of Gorpak and his bullying ways and blunders in judgment, and thoroughly detested the scheming and sneaking ways of Hooka. And, since Borak had ruled them wisely and well during his former term of office,

they welcomed him back warmly. Or as warmly as a
Yathoon can, anyway.

And what about the venomous Fanga, former high
chief of the now-eliminated Garukh clan, I wondered.
Fanga, after all, had cast the vote of the chiefs against
Koja shortly before my skycraft came into view. Was
Koja wise to let a virulent and jealous enemy lurk unslain in the midst of his people, to whisper and con-
spire against him?

I was relieved to hear that Koja had already thought
of the dangers the potential jealousy and rivalry of
Fanga presented. And he had found an unusual but remarkably clever means of mollifying this last of his
enemies.

He had given Fanga the Kandar Clan to rule.

"But—Fanga hates the Kandars!" I protested in bewilderment at this enigmatic and foolhardy step Koja
had taken.

My friend nodded somberly.

"He hates the Kandars," stated Koja solemnly, "because they chose another leader over him, the noto-
rious Gamchan, whom I later slew. The one thing in
the world that Fanga most desired was to become the
high chief of the Kandars, in which Clan he was raised
from cadethood, as was I."

"You mean—?"

"I mean that, for one thing, the Kandars require a
high chief. And Fanga is a high chief without a Clan.
To put the two problems together was to solve both of
them at one stroke. And Fanga has achieved the position he so heatedly desired. He also has the pleasure
of knowing that his successful (and therefore hated)
rival, Gamchan, is dead. Fanga will, I trust, lead the
Kandars well."

"But, Koja-*jan*," young Taran demanded urgently,
"I thought that *you* were the high chief of the Kandars!"

"I was, little Taran," Koja assured him. "But in accepting the throne of the Arkon of the Horde, I gave up the chiefship of the Kandars. According to Horde traditions, the Arkon must foreswear all Clan allegiances. The Arkon of the Horde must forever be a warrior without a Clan, you see; only then can he rule the entire Horde with justice, and be equally fair and equally strict to all of the Clans which compose the Horde. For he must rule impartially, and without favoritism."

Kadar cleared his throat. "I suspect," the lieutenant said, with a wry grin, "that this is more often a goal to be striven for than a rule universally observed."

"Quite so, I fear," Koja agreed. "Perhaps I should have said, a *good* Arkon rules without partiality. And I intend to be a good Arkon."

"And how did Fanga accept this honor?" I inquired.

"With slack-jawed amazement, at first," Koja answered, "for he doubtless expected me to exact a cruel revenge upon him for the malicious vote he cast against me. Then with something resembling a dawning joy. I firmly believe that, in time, he will feel true and honest gratitude toward his Arkon and will become one of my most staunch and loyal supporters, for this would be according to cold reason and logic, and these move the Yathoon heart even more powerfully than do jealousy or hatred, which, after all, partake of the emotional side of an intelligent being's personality.

"And even if I fail in introducing paternal affection and literacy among the Yathoon, and fail in curtailing their bloodthirstiness," he added after a moment of reflection, "it will stand to my credit that, at least, I taught one of them the meaning of gratitude."

"Two of them," Borak corrected him solemnly.

Very shortly thereafter we took our departure. The former captives climbed aboard the *Shondakor* and the little scoutcraft, the *Lankar-jan,* and we took to the air after taking our farewells of Koja and his mate, and of Borak, high chief of the Haroob Clan.

These farewells were brief and cursory, partly because saying good-bye has always distressed me, and partly because they were only temporary farewells anyway. For someday soon, I knew, Koja would ride up before the gates of Shondakor the Golden amidst a mighty retinue of his nobles and warriors, for a visit of state.

We had already discussed a treaty of eternal peace between the Clans of the Yathoon Horde and the Three Cities; if the Yathoon warriors would restrain themselves from raiding the farms and merchant caravans and outlying provinces of Shondakor and Tharkol and Soraba, our fleets and legions would cease attacking them on sight. And we would open avenues of peaceful trade, giving them foodstuffs and weapons and tools and gewgaws in return for the valuable minerals wherewith the Black Mountains were laden.

This concordat, perhaps Utopian, was certainly for the future. But more to be anticipated in the near future was the arrival of Koja and his mate to Shondakor, to introduce to us their firstborn. This he had promised me, and so had Nourya.

And that happy day would perhaps not be too far off, for already—they informed me modestly—Nourya was carrying the eggs she would soon lay. And the gestation period of the Yathoon female is brief, while the larval stage is not much longer.

I wondered if it would be deemed advisable by Koja and his mate to permit Darloona and me the privilege of raising and educating their offspring, at least in part? Koja himself had learned the value and richness of civilization and its arts and gentler ways by living among us: how better to humanize the next generation of the Yathoon and to inculcate the principles of love and friendship and chivalry in their cold hearts than by raising them among humankind?

As for these things, well, we would have to wait and see. The future and its dreams and plans are what make life exciting, and also worth living.

With these thoughts in mind, we flew home under the golden skies.

THE END

Darza, the Chess Game of Callisto

The boardgame of Darza has been played for countless centuries upon Thanator, and its origin has long
since been forgotten.

Like chess or checkers, Darza is played on a board
(called "the field") marked off into alternate dark
and light squares. Whereas chess is played on a board
composed of eight rows of eight squares each, Darza
is played on a field of rectangular shape, divided into
nine rows of seven squares each.

Darza is played with fewer pieces than is chess.
Each team consists of only six pieces, and these teams
are the Ima (the "Reds") and the Chaca (the
"Blacks"). In a complex variation called Akka-Darza,
or "Super-Darza," four teams compete on a field of
nine rows of eleven squares each, but I will not go
into this higher form of the game here.

The names of the pieces, and the variety of moves
they may make, are as follows:

1. *Jan* ("Prince"): Like the king in chess, the
   capture of the Jan is the goal of the game. The
   Jan sits on the midmost square of the last row,

called "Prince's Row," with the rest of the team arranged in an arrowhead formation between the Jan and the opposing team. When played, the Jan can move either vertically or horizontally, for as many or as few squares as the player desires.

2. *Komor* ("Chieftain"): Each team has two Komors, and they sit one row in advance of the Jan and two squares to the Jan's left and right, guarding his flanks. The Komors may be moved horizontally or vertically, like the Jan, but for only three squares at a time. (And, also like the Jan, they may either advance or retreat.)

3. *Thordan* ("Swordsman"): Each team has one Thordan, situated one square to the Jan's left and two rows in advance of Prince's Row. In a perfect coincidence, the Thordan may move in exactly the same way as the knight in chess, that is, he may advance two rows and traverse to the right or the left one square—or move in any similar combination of two and one. The Thordan can also retreat to protect his Prince.

4. *Kordan* ("Bowman"): Each team has one Kordan who stands two squares to the Swordsman's right, on the same row, the third. The Kordan moves only on the diagonal and may traverse as many or as few squares as the player desires. Unlike the Thordan, the Bowman *cannot* retreat, but can only advance.

5. *Vad* ("Scout"): The Vad spearheads the formation and may be moved either to the right or the left, or may advance, but only one square at a time, like the pawn in chess. Also like the pawn, if the Vad of the Imas reaches the Chacas' Prince's Row, the Vad assumes the

powers and prerogatives of a Jan. The Vad
may not be moved backward.

The game of Darza moves much more swiftly than
chess, there being fewer pieces and therefore fewer
options. But it seems to me no less exciting. The design of the pieces varies from elaborate miniature
human figures like statuettes to stylized cones, prisms,
pyramids, pylons, and the like. Generally, the Jan is
represented by a tapering pylon with a medallion on
a chain about its upper part, which probably represents the City Seal worn by royalty. The Komors are
represented by prisms. The Thordan is a cone and
the Kordan a pyramid, while a small sphere on a
rounded base represents the Vad. But these desig-
nations are arbitrary, and variations are commonly
found.

When Super-Darza is played, play moves clockwise
from the opening player. The player of the first move
is decided, much in the earthly fashion, by one player
cupping the Vad of each team in his closed fists and
asking his opponent to name his choice of team; the
opponent will opt, for example, for the Imas, or Reds,
and tap one of the other player's fists. If he has cor-
rectly guessed which color Vad was in that hand,
then he gets the team of his choice and the honor
of making the first move.

Darza means, in literal translation, "war game"; the
term is used to designate a tourney or mock battle,
hence the game is often called Tourney. Some his-
torians of the game are of the opinion that Darza is
a stylized replica of a battle between two squadrons
of warriors, for such squadrons frequently total five
warriors and a squad leader. Others challenge this and
interpret the game on more mystical or symbolic
grounds.

There is, however, no question at all about the

enormous popularity the game enjoys among the several nations of Thanator.

Here follows an illustration showing the Darza field as it looks at the beginning of a game:

THE FIELD OF DARZA

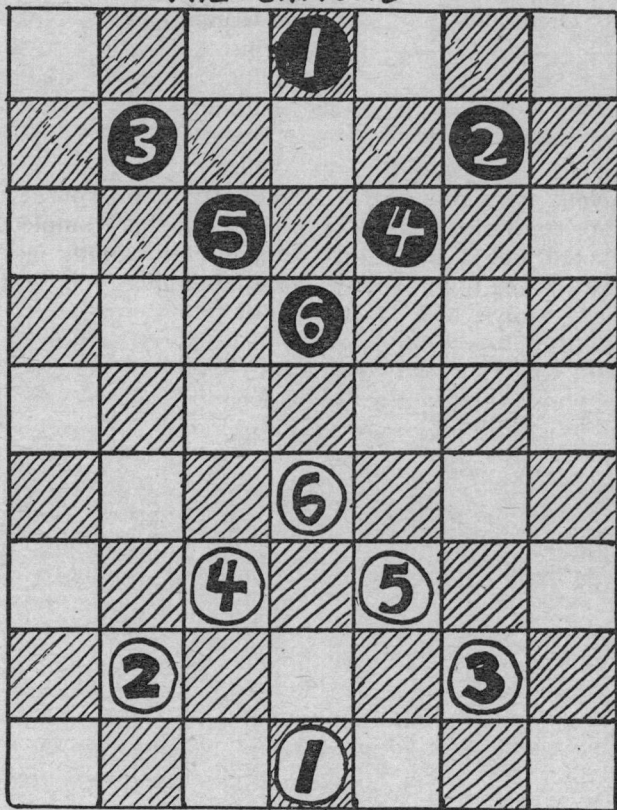

THE CHACAS

THE IMAS

On the field, as illustrated, the numbers represent
the following players on the two teams:

The Chacas	The Imas
1. Kamchan, *Jan*	1. Koja, *Jan*
2. Gorpak, *Komor*	2. Borak, *Komor*
3. Hooka, *Komor*	3. Kadar, *Komor*
4. Gorn, *Thordan*	4. Valkar, *Thordan*
5. Norga, *Kordan*	5. Xara, *Kordan*
6. Orad, *Vad*	6. Taran, *Vad*

END OF THE APPENDIX

Dell Bestsellers